I0739306

USU

Jayde Ver Elst

Printed in the United States of America
First Edition: 2015
eBook ISBN 978-0-9960381-4-0
Softcover ISBN 978-0-9960381-3-3

Published By:
Bad Dream Entertainment®
www.BadDreamEntertainment.com

Cover Illustration by Moa Wallin
www.MoaWallin.com

Cover Design by Leo Ryberg

The 'EyeBrain' logo is a registered trademark of Bad Dream Entertainment, Seattle, WA.
Original trademark design by Darcray - www.Darcray.com

Usu

Prologue

In a time not yet witnessed, there existed a burrow in a junkyard, with only wasteland for scenery. Within this burrow lived a rabbit. This rabbit did not eat, drink, or even breathe... but this rabbit was most certainly alive. And he was the last thing left alive in the world.

Chapter One - The Fall

Usu felt a small weight nestled on the tip of his head which, upon further investigation, turned out to be a rather sneaky blob of what one might commonly call 'snow'. Now, he might have lacked the knowledge of what exactly this 'snow' was, but he still knew well enough that it wasn't something he wanted any part of and so he immediately withdrew his head back into his burrow. Though he did manage a rather wonderful job of teaching the rest of his home the joys of snow while shaking himself clean.

Of course, calling it a home would more than a little generous, considering that it was constructed almost purely from garbage and contained enough sharp pointy bits within it to cause alarm to even the nastiest of antagonists.

However, murderous design faults aside, this was the only home Usu had. More than that, the junkyard itself, steeped in rubble and held tightly by a strong steel fence, was the full expanse of his world. Meager, yet meaningful.

Awkward snow-shaking completed; Usu happened to spot a shimmer of light out of the corner of his eye. The light was reflecting from a small dirt patch near the base of his artificial burrow and curiosity quickly lured our fluffy hero to investigate. He began with a rather despondent nudge at the patch of dirt, as if to tell it that he wasn't really all that interested, but also just enough to not let its hopeful expectations go to waste.

The dirt patch responded in the same way you might expect your average dirt patch to do, it began ticking.

Intrigued, but not willing to give in just yet, Usu gave a slightly stronger nudge than before.

Not to be outdone, the dirt patch began emitting a very slight beep and, considering his lack of experience in the 'being messed with' department, Usu placed his ear as close as he could. The result of the patch feeling vaguely threatened and immediately exploding shouldn't surprise anyone, anytwo, or anythree readers for that matter.

A single thought raced through Usu's mind as he found his body violently sloshing about in an inexplicable mass of dirt, used rubber ducks, and shells of left-over explosive ordnance that were probably not generally approved as construction material:

Bugger

Escape was then his only desire. Escape from this muddy mushroom cloud of brownish yellow and an awfully strange shade of orange, and most of all—most certainly of all—he wanted to be back on solid ground.

His vision began to clear and, with little more than a moment to thank the theoretical gods he had constructed in the junkyard during his spare time (Apollostyrene and Preparation Hades being noteworthy examples), he found himself thirty feet in the air and on a one-way collision course with the unfortunate reality that is—so often—the ground.

Awakening from his five-hour coma, our hero leaped to his feet, knocked debris from his body and took in his new surroundings.

He was in the midst of a city coated in ice, one of the last cities to survive before all life had crawled to an end. Crumbling skyscrapers, decayed sidewalks, and time-worn towers obscured his vision well enough, but a sudden gust of wind shook his new perspective a step further still. It took all his willpower to stay afoot, something the city couldn't quite brag about itself.

Determined to not only figure out exactly where he was, but also how to get the hell away from it, he slowly stepped forward. Usu being our (particularly unlucky) main character, however, tells us that even the act of walking can be filled with arduous perils. This fact was firmly cemented when, moments into his walk, he spotted something digging through a mound of rubble in the distance.

This 'something', as it was just descriptively

referred to, was a large (about five Usu's high and two wide) copper humanoid that appeared to be sorting through the rubble and placing some of it into a mobile furnace attached to its back, pausing occasionally only to complain about 'overtime'.

Relations with this 'something' wouldn't have been so bad if Usu hadn't then made the perilous mistake of shifting his weight onto a particularly noisy piece of paper; one that almost seemed to have been intentionally placed there by a malevolent author attempting to progress the story along. The result was a crumpling so loud, so foul, so nefarious in all its paper-like glory that windows shattered, cars rattled to false life, and our hero, our poor, ever so fluffy hero was set firmly in the sights of a robotic janitorial menace.

Through a brown paper bag oddly attached to what could vaguely be considered its head, piercing eyes began to glow an eerie red, followed only by what appeared to be steam slowly venting out of various joints. Suddenly, it leapt toward Usu, frothing from the closest thing it had to a mouth. Not to be mistaken for a coward however, Usu decided he would stand his ground, only conceding that the ground he would choose to stand on would have to be very, very far away from his current predicament.

Alleyways are nice places. They are particularly nice places when two tons of mobile metal is trying to murder you and your weapon of choice is a pair of fluffy ears. Usu realized this rather early on in his run for dear life, but that realization did little to deter the steaming bastion of metallic hate that had somehow found itself leaping through the air above him during his detailed appraisal of alleyways as escape routes.

Usu jumped forward, rolling with the grace of a Norwegian taxidermist and the guile of a baked potato. Narrowly escaping death, our hero found himself left with no choice but to run inside the first building outside the alleyway. He ran as fast as his padded feet could take him, leaping over rubble and pushing open the somehow-intact glass doors of what seemed to have once been a hotel.

Left alone for less time than it takes to describe, Usu sought refuge in a dimly lit elevator just across from the main entrance. He didn't know many things, but he knew going up was probably a good idea. Unfortunately, his predator felt differently and began climbing the elevator shaft as Usu was in mid-escape.

There's a funny thing about elevators. They're not really designed to have two tons swinging on their cables whilst a stuffed rabbit inside wonders if it is capable of pissing itself or not. I mean, they could be designed for that sort of thing, if they really wanted to be (not to be oppressive or anything), but this one most certainly wasn't. The point was proven when the determined death machine grabbed onto the base of the metal box and caused it to come crashing down on the entire inept cast…

You'd think an elevator without a down button wouldn't have much below it, but then you also think something funny was said a few paragraphs ago and look where that's gotten you in life, you silly thing, you. This elevator was, of course, the exception. So much so an exception that when our fluffy warrior of cowardice awoke amid piles of concrete and a mist of dust, he determined that he was, in his modest calculations, a few hundred miles (in bunny feet of course) lower than he recalled any of the hotel's reception brochures advertising. The brochures in question also weren't quite kind enough to alert him to how his proverbial nemesis was just starting to grumble back to life beneath his feet.

Not to be done in by sheer misfortune, Usu crawled inch by inch out of the wreckage, oft accidentally knocking a rock or two into his pursuer's half-conscious form. This was probably a subconscious attempt to make friends on his part, a bit like when you slowly poison your math teacher over the course of five years because you like math so much, or when you break your wife's leg because she thinks your ideas of ceiling related intercourse are 'unrealistic'. Usu was going to be great at making friends. Presuming, of course, that the fuming hunk of sentient metal behind him wouldn't just use his stuffing for purposes the child-friendly packaging clearly defined as unsafe.

Alas, our hero's attempt at winning hearts through rock throwing appeared to fall on deaf sensors, and before he knew it his escape was thwarted. He now found himself dangling several feet in the air from the arm of a slightly displeased potential murderer. Just as he decided screaming would be a good idea, and just a little bit after he decided having vocal chords and a mouth might make screaming more practical, the fiend reached to Usu's foot, ripped off the piece of paper that had been stuck there since being stepped on and ground a mechanical sigh of relief as he placed it in his mobile furnace unit.

"'You know, if you hadn't run off like that this would have been *awfully* easier on us both," said the still-potentially-murderous-thing with a somewhat resentful tone. "Look, I've been set to auto litter duty for the last few hundred years or so. You know what that's like, right? You're what, a childbot? Petbot? Well, I'm a Modbot. Mod being short for modular and bot short for the boot I'd love to shove up the ass of whoever programmed me."

Usu struggled to find the right words for a response, mostly due to a mixture of awe, confusion, and not having any form of communication ability outside of charades. Yet even still, he was determined to maintain what little peace (and pieces of himself) could be salvaged, proceeding to give an unprecedentedly awkward double-handed thumbs up, with his paws serving as rather large thumb substitutes.

"'You... can't talk? Made in Wales or something? Ah, no matter, I suppose it's easier this way; I argue enough with the sound of just my own voice as things stand." Modbot's casual acceptance was slightly alarming, but considerably less so than him trying to kill our protagonist mere moments ago. "So anyway, I'd wager we fell, what... four hundred feet or so?" Usu nodding in over-zealous agreement. "Then I'd say we'd best start looking for a way out. I've got preprogrammed schedules to keep and you've probably got inanimate objects waiting to attack you, so the sooner we're out of this dank ruin, the better."

Placing Usu down and taking his first steps towards the only passage in sight, Modbot half-heartedly motioned a 'follow me' with one hand, before trudging forward, a floor thick in decay doing little to slow him.

Human - Only

Embrace.

I never thought I'd use that word, at least, at least not this way.

Embraced by a creeping cold, everything fades. Was I right? Will she hate me?

Small hands, a crack to kindle tears, I know I cannot be forgiven, not for this.

The darkness comes, and I force a smile. Teeth rotten with the ache of a simple heart, unable to let go of one selfish wish.

Chapter Two - Sandpaper

Modbot wasn't exactly your everyday garden variety robot. Partially because no one had ever managed to make robots grow from a garden, but mostly because he'd been left on cleaning duty for a century shy of a bigger word. Being modular meant that, with a simple component exchange, he could achieve almost any task, and he most certainly did during the days mankind still pestered about, flies on the dung of the earth as they may have been.

It would stand to reason then, that during the proverbial end-days he'd be set to something especially practical. Reason going the way of humanity, however, left him in charge of trying to clean every nook and granny in sight; the latter being now devoid in populace, of course.

Bitterness set in after the first few decades, and set itself out after a few more. Yet still, bitterly cleaning the ghost of New York City for even one decade was enough for him to artificially develop a plummy accent in defiance. He would spite the once proudly American windows with an unnatural aura of British superiority, whilst forced into making sure they were deliriously shiny.

"And *that* my dear rabbit, is when I discovered the only things left on my hard drive was a Betamax collection of *Monty Python's Flying Circus*, a library of B-grade movies, and a single panoramic session of parliament from when that one chap called that other one a wanker," said Modbot, an estimated four hours into their tunnel walk, Usu wobbling each step forward and using gravity as the occasional head-brake. "You know I... could carry yo—", an offer cut short by an awkwardly segued change in scenery.

Massive isn't quite strong enough a word to describe what lay before them. Exiting the claustrophobic tunnel of A.I. introspection, they found themselves surrounded by obsidian cliffs, an unobstructed view of the sky, and trenches deeper than even the terrain held high. Rickety bridges connected island upon island of struggling land together, dwarfed by a particularly adorned one in the center.

"Ah," Modbot said, taking a few hesitant steps back. "I'm regretting Ding Maps being installed more and more it seems." This certainly wasn't in his records of what underneath New York should look like, or what any city's undercarriage should look like. "Well, they've certainly taken some luxuries with the decor and… whatnot. But let's not let that stop our poorly navigated escape!" Pausing yet again as his gaze found Usu's and, as a result, found itself firmly focused on the largest island, so efficiently foreshadowed in the previous paragraph.

What lay before them was, in the common tongue at the time of construction, called a 'Seriouslygoddamnhugeholyshitweactuallybuiltitand whobrokethespacebar' but was generally shortened to an 'Airship'. An experimental creation at best, it had found itself being feverishly worked on during the last days of humanity's presence, perhaps in the hope that it could have served as a mobile colony. Colossal in size and unthinkable in weight, its thick fusion of iron and wood stood proud as one of the last remaining testaments to the very species that built it. Unsurprisingly, 'Testament' was precisely the name it was personally inscribed with, embossed in solid silver off the starboard bow.

"Testament is it? Now see here my fluffy friend, have you been versed in irony? If so your humor parameters should kick in rather soon; mine did already but they've been dead to me since I read this one book obsessing entirely about single day of the wee-" While Modbot absently monologued onward, Usu was meanwhile transfixed by the sight. It stirred something inside him. Half-images flickered through his mind, each and every one missing its most important piece. They left him with a single soft whisper: "I'll come back for you."

Whatever manner of narrative had held our protagonist hostage was soon dispelled; replaced with a strangely daring zeal. Instead of his usual avoidance of large and potentially murderous objects, Usu began charging toward the airship. Hopping over bridge gaps, swinging through railings, it seemed little would slow down this dash.

"Oh yeah, great, let's all run for the giant death shi—Odd, I thought I had lost sarcasm as well years ago!" Briefly startled by his own ability to say what he didn't mean, Modbot took a noticeably less provoked trudge toward the airship, secretly hoping for a giant arrowed exit sign behind it.

The words Usu heard bound him to his course. Part of him needed this ship, his chest torn in flooding sensations where before he'd known little more than curiosity and fear. There was no time to be afraid, not a moment of lucidity to waste. Granted, that would be easier to take seriously had he not been hopping at the base of the ship for five minutes before his unwilling partner arrived, gave an exasperated sigh, and rather casually peeled back an entire section of ironbark.

"Now look, there are rules about strange places, rules about normal places too, but the ones about strange places are more pertinent here," lectured the anti-climactic refurbished unit as he combed his hard drive for reference. "First, you need to be as quiet, slow, and letha—w-wrong section, sorry. We apparently need to feel around randomly for a light switch of some sort, bump into each other and make suggestively sexual remarks." And, despite being increasingly suspicious of his own help documentation, he took little hesitation with trying to do just that.

Fortunately, Usu had not yet regained a sense of consideration large enough to actually have been present for any part of the conversation. Instead, he was already climbing a staircase his senior in size for even the smallest steps.

Usu finally reached a crack of light and, with all the might you'd expect from a possessed stuffed animal, barely managed to squeeze through it. An effort made slightly less meaningful when Modbot slammed the doors wide open seconds later and sent our hero flying into the nearest deck cavity. Wedged as he was, and uniquely unable to move to little end, Modbot took this as an opportunity to examine the fluffy legs wailing about in what was possibly a performance in some sort of spasmodic Yoga-derived SOS.

It was then when he found the answer to something that had been bothering him since just slightly after he had stopped trying to murder the poor fellow. He found his name.

Stitched on his outer left calf fluscle were the letters 'Usu'; information your humbly omniscient narrator had clearly been in on for quite a few pages now. He began pulling the leg in a vaguely motivated attempt at helping but couldn't help but confirm his suspicions. "So, I take it that 'Oosoo' on your leg is your name? Or… model? Taxidermist?" A cringe-worthy pop released our strangely named protagonist. Leaping to his feet he nodded the most enthusiastic nod you'd see from anything inappropriately medicated, before remembering he had something to do on this ship, something more important than he rightfully understood.

Taking the moment in, and promptly ignoring Modbot's further prodding (both metaphorical and literal) for information, he focused on the after-images that now barely traced his mind. He knew where to go and wasted little time in doing so. Using his trademark not-quite-dead-yet dash, Usu headed to the very back of the deck, entering a small and relatively dank trap-door.

"Right, right, I'm not following you in there. I've got… err, sprockets. They're sensitive. You have fun while I try and actually progress the story along," Modbot could be heard saying as a barely audible mumble from the claustrophobic interior that now stood before Usu. Sparks from dangling cables, the faint smell of diesel, and a layer of thick grease overwhelmed senses that had previously been standing their ground, if only just barely.

Despite this, he took every step forward with determination; a determination to be very, very far away from where he was at present. Five steps, ten, twenty, he'd lost count by the time an almost surreal glow of light greeted his horizon. He could still hear Modbot mumbling to himself up above. Perhaps—he wondered—that's what had kept the robot sane all these centuries. But chances were more likely that a lack of sanity was the reason for the mumbling in the first place.

Stepping into the cerulean light, Usu stood in shock at the forest of terminals that appeared to be its source. Spiraling outward from a single unit, nearly three dozen terminals blinked an ever-patient underscore, waiting for anyone to give purpose to their stagnation. Clothes were draped over some, messages of love and hope scribbled behind others, and shattered screens of desperation hung over a distant few.

The center of the room was dominated by a large curved display which, for reasons apparently unknown to even the author, was currently displaying a closed-circuit feed of Modbot trying to 'modularize' a vacuum cleaner he'd found; an act far less successful than it was anatomically lewd. "Fine, fine! I'll use the hands for a few more hundred years, maybe I'll even find a nice human child's neck to wrap them around! Vacuum would be no good for that, after all," Modbot rattled about bitterly as he tossed aside what was now neither vacuum nor cleaner.

Usu's fragmented memory could help him no further, finding this room inside the behemoth structure was the limit to what had been etched into his heart. Yet it had still taken him to where he needed to be, and with just the right amount of misfortune, he could probably fumble upon what exactly he needed to do next.

He brushed his paws across the nearest screen but, before he could pretend to read even a single word, the darkness claimed him.

Human - Condition

Above me dangled a corpse more alive than any I could scavenge at my feet.

I don't know why I pulled her down, or why she seemed to breathe sweeter air than I'd ever tasted, I only knew she was important.

This clumsy, mumbling, rambling girl; her overflowing humanity made me question my own.

Androids do not dream of electric sheep, they dream of being more than sheep.

She knelt before a lake, peering into the depths, and for all the faults and cruelty in her world she had but one despair:

"I can't see me looking back at me."

Chapter Three - Serendipity

Grasping back at the straws of his cognition, Usu awoke, checked himself for self-urination, checked himself further for thinking he could urinate in the first place, and stumbled to a tragically piss poor variation of 'standing'.

His vision was clouded and in his head permeated a sense of wrongness. Every second, darkness would creep into his skull with a dull ache and a commanding pulse of his heart. Slowly, the pain faded, the darkness waned, and his stance looked less and less like a botched yoga experiment.

He had felt something when he blacked out; an extremely familiar feeling. Memories absent of what he saw or experienced, yet the feeling of a piece of him sliding back into place was undeniable. Hence the bit about making sure he didn't wet himself was only logical you see.

Not far above him sat the console he had so gracefully fallen from a chapter prior. Usu quickly scaled it once more, using two separate disc drives as footholds in the process, finding himself once again staring at his light-source adversary. Before he spent too long convincing himself that his paw print on its thick film of dust meant he got the first hit in, he came to the baffling realisation that he actually understood what was displayed on it. Indeed, when prior to his blackout he was barely capable of admonishing vacuum-cleaner rape, he now possessed the basic computer literacy you've lied about on your CV for years!

He began scouring the system, activating various (and rather audible) functions around him until he froze on a very particular confirmation screen. The words that stalled his largely metaphorical heart were 'Colony A59'. Not quite sure why the ship was involved with multiple colons, let alone naming them in hexadecimal, he wasn't too fond of the idea of pushing the ever-obnoxious OK button that he could swear was growing bigger and bigger across the screen.

Usu was, at least partially, correct about the OK button getting larger. You see, for quite a few moments now, Modbot had been trying to get his attention, presumably to complain about American television or something, an effort that proved increasingly futile. Futile enough that he rationalised, "If he likes that screen that much, he might as well– " before gleefully smashing Usu's head into the screen.

This moment defined many things for our hero, his future, his fear of glowing glass terminals, and most of all, a very good reason to never ignore Modbot from then onward.

Oh, but we mentioned that future bit didn't we? Yes, yes, I suppose that is *vaguely* important at least. You see, Modbot had unknowingly set into motion, delicate irony noted, the force of motion itself. Usu's flailing limbs and the shards of shattered glass were little more than a distraction now that the whole world seemed shake, and a roar bellowed through every inch of their beings. Then, much like if one were to use a teapot to substitute binoculars, they both had a rather sudden and literal change of perspective, as they were sent flying from one corner of the room to another.

With the eloquence of a bewildered walrus, Modbot screamed with each shift, changing to a noticeably deeper pitch whenever he faced Usu or any number or inanimate objects he had yet to have his way with. Usu, on the other hand, was still struggling to come to terms with nearly being murdered and barely noticed his cushion-based body flopping about. He was dedicating most of his attention to giving an evil eye to Modbot, with the rest of his resources trying to figure out how to apologise for said evil eye once they stop their synchronised smashing.

The world around them wasn't entirely oblivious to this course of events either. As it turned out, not only did the ship launch, but it ripped up the few dozen islands it had been tethered to in the process. The chains that did said tethering were now whipping field-sized hunks of earth through the air as momentum continued to gain. I could use a metaphor or simile to describe the amount of damage done by this, but instead I'll suggest you put all that useless coin change of yours into the microwave, set it to a good five minutes or so, and stare very, very closely.

Those of you still alive to finish reading this paragraph can now begin regretting it, as you are forced to use your imagination to grasp the full extent of the destruction left in their wake.

Five minutes. Five long grueling minutes inside the most well-varnished washing machine you could imagine was *roughly* how long it took for gravity to high-five them into the floorboards, a welcome release from the ceiling at this point. There was now a stable, comforting hum not entirely unlike flying transportation would be expected to produce. Dozens of turbines, and a baker's worth of gravity inverters held the skyward beast aloft, all remnants of the anchoring chains now ground into a long-passed dust.

Having escaped the room they would spend the bad half of a chapter in, Usu and Modbot stumbled onto the deck and were immediately hit with enough air-force to nearly combine the two. Modbot desperately tapped away at a button just outside the door until finally, with a victorious whinge, worn glass panels raised from each side, doing a somewhat naughty-looking interlocking ritual at the top.

The air settled and so did they. Now able to take in the scenery without becoming part of it, Usu was wide-eyed at the world shifting past him. Every now and then he'd hop a few times and drag Modbot to explain something mundane like a Tower-of-Dead-Bankers, and somewhere in that cynical copper head the robot began to appreciate it, even taking a portion of pride in having a use beyond cleaning after dead humans.

"Look, that's the thirtieth Tower-of-Dead-Bankers we've passed now. I explained already that they all made very good building material by not having souls, but every building is built on a firm foundation of bankers. They'd spent centuries holding onto other people's money, so they were considered best for the role of holding onto other people's bodies." Modbot's final sentence, the rare type that only questioning could make you seem like a bigger tosser than the one saying it in the first place, was followed by, "It's all simple logic you know."

Logic, being out for tea at that moment, could not be brought in for further comment.

Other schools of thought, however, notably sanity, did decide to weigh in on the matter. You see, Modbot's somewhat bitter disposition against organic life in human shape had him taking advantage of Usu's curious bewilderment. The towers in question were not in fact flung together corpses, but rather, gigantic stone monoliths that served as shelters for anyone brave enough to travel on foot in the past. Artificial oxygen had been generated inside by synthetic flora, a desperately needed pit stop at the time.

Modbot did, however, have a few points right; the majority that could not settle for a life in the colonies without giant screens yelling advertisements or stock indexes respectively, were indeed marketers and bankers. Though their well-dressed corpses had merely littered the monoliths, rather than having been the foundation for them.

Just then, in the loudest silent shrill only a mute rabbit could possibly pull off, Usu pointed rapidly. "That? That's…That's a junkyard. Scrapheap." Generating a small sarcastic holographic rainbow from his fingertips, he finished, "The place all of us robots dream of malfunctioning in for eternity!"

It wasn't Usu's junkyard they saw as they sped past overhead, it was simply that he hadn't known any existed other than the one he called home. For a moment, he wondered if there were others like him in each one, then he looked at Modbot and wondered if there were more of those too.

Enthusiasm then abruptly went out for a few donuts.

Human - Attachment

Something stirred inside me, a witch's elixir for a dying world laid bare a seed of hope, but instead I found rage.

It won't work.

It won't solve anything.

This massive, hulking beast we seek to flee on.

I won't leave. I won't forsake her.

This girl who feels every stroke of fate's brush and bares every strike of its cruel whip with a smile.

She is our real hope or, perhaps at least, mine.

Chapter Four - Frankincense

Making a habit of passing out is a bit like making a frozen yogurt; both could pass for pleasant under the right circumstances, but you'd probably want neither several hundred feet in the air, mere minutes before a dreadfully climactic scene. Usu had not the luxury of choice. It was brief however, barely taking any time to recover at all, though that might have been because Modbot had caught him, perhaps out of an ever so slight guilt about smashing his face into a glass screen panel earlier on. However, confessions not being legal tender meant this was probably as much admittance as you'd ever get from a robot forced not to harm humans, but seemed to be doing a stunning job at harming other things.

Clearly competing for the role of narrator, an over-powering female voice now reverberated around them. "DOCKING PROCEDURE IMMINENT" was the polite way of the navigational system saying it was going to gracefully slam into a nearby structure, a feat it did rather well, presuming it intended to keep a flight record of zero survivors. The monstrosity tore through what may well have been up to nine different layers of sheet metal and concrete before finally settling gently down next to a bare-boned staircase that lead into the heart of the massive structure they had just bored into with smashing grace. Worn decals reading 'A59' littered the twisted metal haphazardly strewn together to comprise the structure's interior.

Of course, calling it a structure for god knows how many paragraphs wouldn't be right. Instead, we'll call it what it really was, a large colony built into the Rocky Mountains. What met the eye alone surpassed street-variety imagination, but in reality so much more was hollowed out beyond immediate sight, reaching depths we'd rather not start putting math against. This was the very same colony whose mere name had triggered Usu's first of many awkward black-outs, and yet he still had only the smallest of inclinations as to why; perhaps a side effect of the immense brain damage being smashed head-first into a glass panel tends to give you.

"Blimey balls and blue-arsed flies!" instinctively muttered Modbot, his British sectors notably flustered by the ship's very vague interpretation of the word 'docking'.

He'd made a lovely dent in the only useful door during the impact, and was briefly compelled by his programming into cleaning up his own mess before the ship had the audacity to insist, "DOCKING PROCEDURE SUCCESSFUL" at which point he, ignoring the ever-wobbly Usu examining the smash-related-entrance, delved into a twelve minute rant about how he doubted this ship had the wits to dock with an iPod. The ship, having not been established as a sentient character, failed to answer his taunts, and instead slowly fell silent as its every mechanical inch sank back into dormancy.

"Ugh, these things never listen, and when they do they just blame it on being programmed precisely like actual pilots, including the drunk ones it seems. Now you, Usu, at least you show some colour when cha—" It was only then that he noticed that he, irony be damned, couldn't quite notice Usu anymore. After taking a few long moments to peer into every nearby vent and to perhaps *relatedly* check up on a certain vacuum cleaner, he was fairly sure the fuzzy rodent wasn't on the ship anymore. What made him absolutely sure was the tiny bit of fluff at the steel stairwell they'd landed next to, and the odd way it seemed to form an arrow before he dutifully incinerated it.

Feeling slightly dejected at having both his indignant rant with the synthetic voice and his appeasement through flowering camaraderie denied, Modbot was at a rare junction in his existence. He could, theoretically, smash his own face in the control room until he hopefully got sent to some slightly more familiar destination, at which point he could resume his joyous days of bitterly cursing humanity as he cleaned up after them. He could also follow the extremely subtle fluffy arrow, and no doubt get caught in a fate spun of numerous exploding things, smashy things, and rather difficult make-shift sign language interpretation.

Noble a bot as he was, the choice was simple, or at least made simple after he checked several dozen times that the entire flight system had become as extinct as those who made it. He would foster this blossoming friendship, and at least pretend it was by pure intention. He set his leg servos to a 'moderately annoyed' speed for the first time in decades as he crawled through the hanging gardens of broken glass and barbed metal. Standing once more on the other side, he took note that he was on the small stairwell, measuring perhaps only four Usus wide and surrounded by a gargantuan hollow wind tunnel. The door in front of him was already open, a clearer sign he couldn't ask for.

Immediately upon stepping foot in the building his senses, which had previously been dulled by the howling air from moments ago, were now privy to a rather obnoxious dripping noise. He hated dripping noises. Everyone did. But everyone, as you may recall, was currently preoccupied with being dead and thus had not the luxury of finding the source, let alone solving such an obvious hydro-disaster in the making. "No, no, I've… I've got to find the little bugger thing, there's no doubt he's causing all manner of other havoc!" Modbot did little to sway his own judgment, even with such despondently passionate words. "Oh fine, fine, fine! He probably started the drip! Or he's at the drip! We always planned on re-uniting at drips if we were lost didn't we?!" And so his course was set in bi-pedal motion. Modbot would use centuries of refined research at the pinnacle of human science to try and find a leaky spot, and Usu, well he had something quite different in store for him.

From the very moment he entered, Usu was overcome with an overwhelming feeling of panic.

Hysteria of a nature few ever come to feel, for he was not afraid of what might be ahead, but far, far more afraid of what might not be. Every step he took came with an image, every second step a voice from memories long buried. Carrying himself through countless passages until, in one derelict room, he finally came to a standstill before a single shaft of sunlight piercing the beautiful porcelain shell of a girl.

Silence took him, no images, no voices. White noise seemed to have taken the place of kaleidoscope of resurfacing images, and moments before he shut his eyes, giving in to another bout of unplanned unconsciousness, he was—rightfully—surprised to hear a series of banging noises followed by "Yeah! Fuck you, leaky pipe dripping all ov—I mean… Good show Sir pipe but you've lost this duel!" Which made all the drama before it seem a little silly.

He was awake now and aware enough to see the

figure crouched in the sunspot, a figure that was likely the entire reason he was here at all. Before him was the shape of a poorly dressed girl, no older than ten. Her thin frame wrapped around itself as if she was afraid to let herself go, whilst her back arched toward the light. Thin glass panels drinking a rich meal before tapering at each end, wing-like enough to make a fairy of lore feel inadequate.

Long dark brown hair spun on the floor around her, each strand beaming with a vitality that poorly matched her pale tone and vacant eyes; like coal snuffed before it burned brightest. She had been there for many, many lifetimes, and our dear Usu had made her wait. He took a step, yet nothing gave way, he took two more and the results were the same. Like any who would have seen the same sight he did, he could not resist approaching her proper, and gently tracing his right paw across her mouth onto her cheek.

Solitude gave way.

Eternity cracked.

And a little girl's lips moved in sync with a heart she could never prove existed.

"I missed you so much."

As if injected with life itself, the machination began shaking and slowly but surely rose into a standing position as a layer of porcelain dust slipped free of her frame and wafted into the air around them. Her eyes were no longer that of the dead, but held a gentle flame that looked down at our protagonist with a pure warmth. Usu, being experienced only in things trying to kill him, however, reacted by jumping a foot back, immediately turning around, and running with his arms flailing above his head.

She wasn't confused, or even surprised; she'd long ago spent enough time on pointless emotions already. The girl chased him with a speed he'd never even imagined, corridor after corridor they ran and, sanity notwithstanding, she began to smile and even giggle.

Then, just before being forgotten in the narrative

altogether, Modbot rather inconveniently stepped into Usu's path. "Oh god, why are you runnin—*phpohsppphhh!*" The last bit being an onomatopoeia best representing the sound Usu made as he slammed into Modbot's chest. The one that shortly followed as the girl slammed into the both of them is better left to the imagination, however.

The crumpled mess on the floor was not still for long. The pursuer had already grabbed Usu in both of her arms and was holding him toward the ceiling as she rolled happily on the ground.

"Sssnooow! You came back! You promised Rain and you came!" Her eyes filled with delight, Usu could no longer be scared of this girl. Her wings, solar panels of an emerald nature, fluttered and a smile brighter than any sight he had seen drew itself on her face.

This was but a normal little girl, and because of that, the most beautiful thing he'd ever seen.

Cranking his crankables back into a somewhat

less cranked state, Modbot couldn't wait until he was standing before giving this little scenario a piece of his pre-approved conversation dictionary. "Now see here Miss… Miss… well, an android I presume? It's all good and jolly that you're good and jolly, but I think you might have a case of mistaken identity. This little ruffian is named Usu and is almost certainly not this 'Snow' fellow."

"Silly shiny-thing! Usu is a dolly, Snow is a boy, aaand Rain is happy!" rebuked the cheerful little humanoid.

"Shinything?! Well, thank you kindly for noticing; polish is dreadfully hard to find in post-post-apocalyptic times, and is very rare I'll have you know!" Pausing briefly to regain some composure "Your name is… Rain I take it?"

"'Rain is Rain!"

"'Yes well, either I'm right or you're the worst weather channel replacement they ever built." Feeling his pride slowly setting back into place as he put others in theirs, he continued. "You see Miss

Rain, we got a little lost and then I got a little violent, and then we got a little more lost and… and then this little guy somehow got us here. When you've stopped shaking his unconscious pre-corpse, I'd think we'd both appreciate if you could tell us how to get out of here? Or maybe even just where exactly *here* is?"

Pointing to his conveniently lit up chest display, "You see, I'm getting a reading that we're somewhere near Utah. Usually with Ding maps this means I'd be lost somewhere in Asia, yet I don't recall crossing any oceans before we 'docked' so effortlessly through several layers of metal and rock arguably less dense than the navigation system."

Rain only glimpsed at his worn but suspectly clean display for a moment. "Rain hasn't really been outside before, but is pretty sure that's here!"

Choking briefly at her enthusiasm, Modbot gave his most gleeful reply. "Oh Christ, do you have any idea what Utah is like now?! It's– well, the same as it always was; desert, and not the good kind!" He was hiding his fear of deserts rather well for someone who just yelled in terror about it, when he took a sip of lubricative oil and wiped some purely dramatic sweat off his forehead.

Human – Being

Fumbling hands and frustrated whispers, a secret most would fear.

But instead, a gift.

Small and fragile, not unlike herself, a stuffed rabbit was to be my boon.

I held them both close, she didn't understand, and somewhere inside, I hoped she never would.

Chapter Five - Period

As far as mountainous end-of-days-we're-all-going-to-die structures went, Colony A59 ranked rather well during its peak, if only because all of the municipal rating sheets had long since been used as a toiletry solution by the more desperate residents. Self-approval ratings had at all times been at an all time high, with not even one council member declaring themselves fit for molecular disassembly. Indeed, Colony A59 was almost as highly ranked as its namesake, coming in just behind 'David's Washing Machine' when it came to places survive in a world whose atmosphere had thinned so drastically that oxygen was a commodity.

Few saw it coming, fewer still listened. Mother nature no longer intended to nurture a doomed race, and with them everything withered until you couldn't find a blade of grass or a speck of algae. The only things remaining of once-proud humanity were their shelters and their artificial slaves, most unable to comprehend the freedom they inherited afterwards. Yet, in time settlements grew, teachings emerged, and the creatures created to serve under mankind had all but replaced them.

Modbot and Rain were just two examples. Modbot, built to serve any need, and Rain, a prototype made to ease the broken hearts of those who lost their real children to the hardships of a dying world.

However, much like real children, Rain lacked the delicate restraint necessary to *not* throw Usu up and down into the ceiling as she merrily walked along familiar corridors, now coated in the ash of bones.

"Why is a big strong shinything like you afraid of deserts anyway?" muttered rain as she collected Usu's corpse from the thirtieth ceiling fist-pump in one half-hour.

"Listen girl, firstly it's Modbot. The shine takes effort, I thank you again for noticing, but my eyes are up here!" Clearing his imaginary throat before continuing onward, "As for deserts, they're dreadful things! Hot enough in the day to boil your oil, cold enough at night to seize your gears. Worse yet, in cleaning mode I'm likely to recognise the whole thing as 'dusty' and be stuck cleaning *that up* for a few more centuries!" He grabbed his chest to calm an equally imaginary heart. "Yet I know we—or at least I—must endure. The closest chronicle is Old Francisco, built around the entirety of the Golden Gate Bridge."

Rain, notably as absent minded as Usu was about the current era, followed up with the rather logical question, "Chronicle? You want to visit a book?"

Modbot sighed once more at the fact she wasn't a real little girl he could strangle, and instead answered "No no, Chronicles are... are... they're like this but made up of things like us. There's probably some form of transport available from them, at least I hope so; I never did visit the one in New Jersey. That place, lass, has a history of filth not even I could clean up."

You, dear reader, already robbed of whatever time and money you used to get this far, would likely be questioning the choice of 'Old' Francisco as opposed to the more historically ironic 'Sans' right about now. Allow your narrator to elaborate that there was indeed a period where the name did bear a startling resemblance to that; unfortunately that period was marred by most of the creative robots not having committed accidentally assisted suicide. They had, in confused honour of their missing masters, chosen 'Comic Sans Francisco'. This name lasted for an entire week before the mass (but clearly accidental) suicides adjusted things appropriately. It's suspected one or two creative robots may still be functioning, mysteriously appearing coffee foam designs are proof enough of that, but the likelihood of them trying to name a city after a font again is… highly unlikely.

Like two gears clicking into motion, Rain placed Usu on the floor near her time-tattered feet and, summoning the guile one would expect from anything above a goldfish, exclaimed, "You want to go outside?!" Her eyes made mechanical sounds that defied her human image as they expanded in dilation.

"Well, yes. I've got a few more hundred years left and might just manage to clean out a bistro or two in that time, and this little guy, he seems to really like junkyards. Probably stays near one where we positively did not try to murder each other, and by each other I may mean just him."

Sounding more nostalgic than her makings would confess, Rain replied, "Snow doesn't like junkyards, he just didn't have a choice. Sometimes he'd smile when talking about them thou—" Rain's goldfish senses awakened once again to interrupt herself. "You want to take him with you? Boo! Snow is not going anywhere without Rain! Boo Modshiny, boo!"

Usu, had been standing between the two for some time now, left largely to wonder how a conversation about him, and furthermore, surrounding him, managed to completely ignore his presence, input, and general existence. Of course, not possessing a mouth, speaker system, or means of communication other than bouncing hysterically—which he was now doing in earnest—were probably primary culprits.

"Shush, shush you, I'll check your danger diaper in a moment," Modbot said, dismissing Usu's clamour for existential recognition. "More importantly, I think we need to get you out of this mistaken identity cliché. You see, girl," turning to face Rain once more. "It appears you're mistaking our surprisingly squishy little rabbit robot here for an *actual live human*. Allow me to remind you that his name, Usu, is rather poorly stitched into his leg. Oh, and I suppose all living creatures being dead, most notably here *humans*, for the last three-hundred years, well that might be important as well." Modbot had seized a logical victory, one no one could argue against, one that made perfect sens—

"Boo!" Retorted Rain, in a surprisingly effective one-word maneuver.

"'No no, you can't just shout 'Boo!' every time you don't like something; that isn't debate, and I'd wager it isn't even a good haunted house substitute coming from you."

Grabbing Usu with both hands and holding him close to her chest, Rain spun in a circle and when she next faced Modbot firmly declared,, "They're the same! I know he doesn't feel like Snow, and he doesn't smack me on the head nearly as much, but he's the same. Usu is the dolly Rain made for Snow, but... Usu didn't move back then. I think so at least, it hurts a little to remember."

"Gods girl, it's no wonder they made so few of your kind. You really believe the words coming out of your mouth don't you?" Exasperated, Modbot continued. "Ah, fine. I'm the only one here with a real objective, even if it was programmed into me by sadists, so I'll be off to that absolutely lovely desert boiling around us." Leaning in close to Usu he mumbled, "It's been fun, or something like it at least," before giving him what could only be considered a 'good luck' flick to the forehead.

Fleeting moments make good postcards, but this post-apocalyptic era had little need for them, or mailmen for that matter. All it took were those moments for Modbot to be gone, a noticeable clank of the airlock for confirmation. Usu didn't know if he had found his place, or just lost it. He only knew that the hands that cradled him and the eyes that seemed to cherish him were important and more than just a piece in the puzzle.

Time, from that moment forward, seemed to stand still; Rain would spend days telling him about all the things she had imagined they could do when they met again, but every time she tried to recall things they had already done together a pain seemed to warp her small frame. Sometimes she would abruptly pause for hours, frozen in place, and it was those hours when Usu truly felt alone. A feeling he had never felt before leaving his walled-off world at the provocation of a poorly written bit of plot involving explosive ordinance; why now did he feel it? Why was a desperate war being waged within him? Feelings were fighting to the surface. Emotions long lost and memories more important than their poor use of foreshadowing would suggest.

The days they spent together seemed to move painfully fast. Games like 'See how hard Snow can fly into the ceiling' broken by that strange, sudden stillness about her, each time robbing her of a small but precious moment. Usu would shake her body, pull her limp arms, but only time—that very same beast that took her from him—would bring back this sweet, accidentally violent on purpose girl.

Soon, Usu had regained enough memories, or at least their impressions, to understand that Rain was far from well, that even the shadows in his memory would not play such a cruel joke.

His mind cleared for an instant one day when she stood suspended in one such moment of stillness, and he finally grasped the fear assailing him, only to wish away the truth revealed. Rain was not simply unwell.

She was dying.

Human - Empathy

She lost another one today, another moment to oblivion.

Our first encounter, a smile to hide what was no longer within her.

Now she holds a diary, maybe something like this.

But with happier thoughts I hope, an ever more endearing refrain.

She doesn't deserve this, I would take it all if I could.

And if any Gods are listening, in time, I will.

Chapter Six - Nostrum

Death's meaning had become blurred in a world where, by the grace of an anorexic atmosphere, nothing was rightfully alive anymore in the first place. Even more so, the 'life' of an android in such a world shouldn't have held any weight, and it shouldn't have meant anything to anyone, but one did. Her survival was paramount to one, and that very desire for it was the only thing strong enough to bind a soul to a world that had long since rejected its own creations.

Usu had realised he was unnatural for some time now; it didn't take a girl joyously slamming him into random objects to grant that perspective, nor did it take the identity crisis of being called by a name clearly different from what he had sewn into him. It was seeing Rain slowly fall apart which latched onto the emptiness inside him, and suddenly, he wanted to save her more than anything. Yet as fate would have it, stuffed rabbits are not blessed with especially high technical skill-sets, despite what an inflated CV might insist on telling you.

Scouring the library produced little, mostly because of there not being one at all, but at least partially because what he was looking for wasn't an answer just any tome could contain. Androids differed from robots deeply; whereas one was built to slave away in a human's stead, the others were built to replace them entirely. Comfort for souls in solitude. But as with many things, the success of their design brought about their own demise. Mankind rejected the false life, despised the empathetic machinations, and even in her era of origin Rain was one of the only androids to survive. Mass-butchering had been a distracting carnival of hate to allow humans to briefly ignore what awaited them. They could finally blame someone other than themselves, they could curse someone other than their gods, and they could kill beings capable of profound emotion yet bound to not fight back.

These memories came back to Usu in bits, pieces, and the occasional trolley to the head. The trolley was usually Rain slamming him on something and then immediately hugging him, an act so lacking in malice that most would gladly receive lasting brain damage to endure. She had good reasons most of the time, often preempting such an experience with "Bunnycoaster! Whooosh—Wall!" or "Flyyyyyyy!". And yes, she pronounced the extra y's. All of them.

Her spirits certainly weren't lacking; she'd waited hundreds of years for anything close to this, after all. Rain spoke from her heart or didn't speak at all. This policy somewhat contrasted with Usu's policy of having no mouth, something that was starting to cause him an awful lot more trouble than when all he had to worry about were weather conditions. Still, he knew the answer to saving her wasn't in the colony; they'd spent a week there and he'd found about as much useful information as a spice merchant's thesis on water-boarding.

Usu needed to get answers, to get Rain checked before her time stopped again, or worse still, his fears made flesh at the behest of eternity's whims.

With as little as he knew about the world as it was, he could only rely on Modbot, or at least his shadow. He'd help, he knew he would; he'd moan about it a lot, but he'd still do it.

Now, explaining the need to travel to Rain was the real challenge at paw. He hadn't had much success explaining the lack of necessity in putting ribbons around every object in order to 'Loop of pretty!' them. Or at least that's what his every limb—now having a ribbon attached—would claim. But this time! This time he was marginally more prepared. He had in his possession both a permanent marker, a large white-board, and one seat facing it. He'd chosen an old AV club room in the school district, pubescent smells thankfully absent.

After much animated coaxing, Usu motioned

her into the room where his plan was carefully scribbled out.

"You want me to go in there? Okay, Snow but..." she said, looking down at her bare feet to gather determination. "If this isn't ending in a cuddle, Rain is going to give you one anyway!" Her affectionate protest largely ignored, she came in and glanced to the upside-down bucket that substituted a proper chair. Preparations had been perfect up to this point, minus Rain putting him on the seat instead, placing the entire white-board on his lap, and insisting he 'paint her like one of his French girls'.

Another half an hour of vehement charades later, Usu finally managed to situate both the girl and the whiteboard properly, an accomplishment nothing short of a miracle. She tilted her head, first diagonally, and then horizontally at the board. Then, as if trying to make out a psychological inkblot, she quizzically posited, "Three birdies and half a choo-choo?" Needless to say, this particular drawing was *not* of three birds and half a train, but rather a crudely constructed map of the local area, with helpful arrow markers that cunningly pointed to other arrow markers in case she got lost.

Usu shook his head and traced across the map from arrow to arrow, a feat requiring several bunny hops to cover the distance. He then finally tapped his paws rapidly on the destination Modbot was supposed to have gone, Old Francisco.

"You want to go there too? You and Shinybot can't be… more than just friends can you? Rain doesn't know how to be a rival!" said the clearly flustered girl before bonking herself on the crown of her head and winking. "Well, if Snow goes, I go. Have to keep watch and make sure bad-bads don't get you. Or Shinybot either!" she concluded before commencing to scribble something estranged in a worn diary she always seemed to have on hand. "No peeking! Diary peeking is very boo!"

Saying he was surprised at how easily he got her to agree, albeit through the false premise of androsexual rabbit-modbot love, would be an understatement of some calibre. He had assumed she'd be more attached to her home of the last few centuries, or at least more aware of his intentions, but what mattered was his success. Now, there was at least a chance he could save her from whatever ate her away from the inside. It's also worth mentioning that there were considerably fewer walls outside to be happily smashed into; this may be considered to have played at least some part in his reasoning.

Originally intending to leave immediately, they would instead leave first thing in the morning; the result of a brief change in plans caused by Rain's tackle-hug-nap-time-attack, a move largely barred from professional wrestling. Every night there was amateur night however, and he had little in ways or means to protest. For the most part though, Usu had long since stopped caring about the injuries that came with her affection, instead he was happy to spend any time near her at all, time he was well aware she could not afford to waste, time she may not even remember, which made it all the more precious despite.

Morning came as it always does, sun piercing the sky and warping the few fragments of oxygen it could find. A particularly normal morning with absolutely nothing noteworthy being said about it. As Rain stood there, the airlock doors stuttering open to a world she'd seen even less than than our protagonist, it was necessary to mention that she had decided to tie Usu's limbs to a fishing pole for 'fast times!', or so the explanation from her went, after the entire process was already completed at that.

Her words did have merit; few things on the planet moved as slow as Usu, and fewer still faster than a bipedal android. She strapped a belt tightly across her waist and forced the pole through the smallest of crevices to secure Usu as best she could. Rain took a moment to try and hug him but her own innovation had placed his dangling bunny corpse barely out of her reach, so she got on with her nonsense instead. She leaned forward, one knee to the ground, and before even looking to see if the shutter had completely opened, she leaped using a single foot, rendering any further talk of the shutter too traumatic for the shutter's family or close friends.

It should also be remembered that Colony A59 was nestled high in the Rocky Mountains and her momentous leap made gravity pause for thought, before rightly remembering she's got to come down at some point and that it had best get to enforcing that bit lest someone see it slacking.

The laws of physics awoke from their nap to send her shuttling down to the very base of the mountain range, having her single leap move them from the heart of Utah to the edges of Nevada. As she was falling, she asked, "Snow, which way now?" Usu, barely holding his bearings, starred deeply into the map print-outs he'd made the night before and gestured with his head westward.

Rain landed, and the barren soil beneath her shattered all too slowly for her to notice as she instantaneously began running. This was a different beast entirely and a large reason why people had feared them enough to decorate walls with white blood and scattered circuitry, but for the time being a means to an end, or rather, a means to preventing an end. If he needed to use what condemned Rain to save her, he would a thousand times over.

Speaking of thousands; meters and miles flew past Usu barely slower than they had in the airship, and if it wasn't for the haunting moments in which she would pause completely, he might have come to doubt there was anything wrong with her at all. In what seemed like a blink of a rather wind-burned eye, they were already half-way through Nevada, and in another equally blistered blink, Rain froze in time just as they reached the eastern edges of Lake Tahoe.

Usu, having shat several lifetimes worth of

proverbial pants, decided it was as good a time as any to have a break. He wrestled his arms free and tore the map off of himself before examining Rain more closely. It was just like all the other times; eyes usually filled to no end with vibrancy now lay vacant instead. Nothing would wake her up, nothing he could do at least, and he'd tried an awful lot of things at that. Whatever it was that would take her from the world was the only thing that would bring her back, and he had little choice but to wait.

Of course, 'little choice' is different than 'no choice', so on a writing technicality Usu explored his surroundings. He noted the massive lake Rain just barely had not killed him in; water more gray than blue, perhaps to mirror the shells of trees and landscape of ash which surrounded it. The distance littered itself with recreational ruins, hotels and lodges reduced to little more than rubble, and yet somehow still offering competitive rates, at least as far as rubble accommodation typically went for. A world of monochrome encapsulated them both, free from the chaos of old but further still from any joy.

Only monoliths stood solid in the furthest distances, begging to pierce the skies for the slightest salvation. The dead that littered them found no God for that cause, nor a mortician.

Then, for a moment it seemed as if the world fought back, and a shell-shock inducing crash of thunder shook our hero's already wobbly foundations even further.

Human – Pride

Bloodied from tip to toe, and I doubt a drop isn't my own.

Wounds to lick and sprains to heal.

Spurred on by the stares of hatred and howls of disgust that marred our path.

Am I so cruel to protect her? Am I wrong to stop those who would see her suffer?

It didn't matter.

Long ago, I had already learned; gravestones do not fight back.

Chapter Seven - Stitch

Rain's namesake was far from a mere coincidence of poorly written fiction; instead, it was something she chose for herself shortly after the day Snow carried her out of a slightly upper-class colony scrap heap. At first, she would barely talk; a condition he soon missed. In time, a strange form of bond was born between the two, both cast out as dregs of society, yet ever intertwined in fate's firmest clasp.

She had wanted a name like his, a name that would bring her closer to him, she wanted to be what helped Snow become Snow.

It was a beautiful theory, marred only by her ignorance of what rain had truly become. The days where it was little more than an excuse to claim that your vibrating umbrella was not of a sexual nature were long gone. Acid and sulfur had since made it their malevolent home.

This, like most things thus far and probably still

ahead, Usu learned first-hand. The sound of thunder frightened him, the proceeding drizzle confused him, and seeing larger drops of the caustic precipitation start to eat away at Rain's skin terrified him into action. He'd done well to have spotted a cave not far off, even if the endless tourist signs directing him to 'Cave Rock' certainly made it an easy find. With little regard to any effect the rain was surely having on his own body, he immediately grabbed the fishing rod still tightly tucked into her belt and began dragging her to cover. His paws would slip, his face would get muddy, and he was sure he'd passed bits of himself floating in puddles, but this was all he could do for her.

He persisted for an overly dramatized fifteen entire meters before the rod snapped at the mouth of the cave. Yet still he did not pause; he grabbed her lifeless arm and pulled her further and further inward until only her feet were left exposed to the elements. Usu, at a loss for strength but not resolve, laid his body across them as the darkness once again embraced his world.

Liquid pelted his face and something like sirens wailed helplessly in the distance. When Usu finally opened his eyes, he found Rain hunched over him crying, desperately threading closed the tears in his body, with little pause to berate his actions. "Not again, Snow! You can't leave me again, you can't… I can't…" Waxing and waning hysterically, she eventually noticed he had come to, and simply held him close. They laid there for hours as the world slowly melted around them.

Do not mistake this scenario, dear reader, for a lover's tryst; Usu was gaining memories as fast as Rain was losing them, but neither understood the obscure concept of romance. Usu only understood that he wanted to keep her safe, to keep her as she was and Rain, Rain simply wanted to be near him. There are feelings above and beyond what humans would ever understand, but fortunately all those pesky critters had long since been washed away.

Steeling herself, vaguely ironic because of any steel she might have contained inside her, Rain continued her now less frenzied repairs. Bringing a sewing kit with her from the colony was smart, the same one she had used to make Usu, smarter still. What wasn't quite so smart was Usu flinching while being stabbed, necessitating Rain to squeeze his neck between her arm and thigh to keep him still. Times like this make your humble narrator glad he lacks an actual voice, audio book version notwithstanding, and therefore doesn't have to put on airs about ridiculous sounding noises like 'Ugughgghhgwgfh' and such.

He is, however, contracted by obscure literary laws, required to tell you still more.

They weren't far now, even Usu's crushed skull could see the gold gate's skeleton in the distance, along with the mechanical deviations still twisting it to life. He'd hoped they might have run into Modbot on the way there; his world felt small enough to entertain the thought at least, but considering that it had been weeks between departures, he had little surprise for once.

Of course, time did not stand still for either. Whilst Usu looked to save Rain and wound up underneath Cave Rock, Modbot didn't have the luxury of a hundred meter-jumping girl to ride on. Instead, his journey had been a grueling one from the onset. It took him days alone to descend, a few more to complain about having to do it at all, and a sparse one in-between to comment about the Queen in a desperate bid to secure his artificial British trappings.

Worse yet, as his assisted-by-the-assisted GPS system had long pointed out, he took a long route through desert terrain, made only more hellish in this era. He may not have been able to feel heat in the most basic sense of touch, but he was extremely capable of being annoyed by his temperature monitor screaming at him neigh constantly. Fortunately, he was also at least somewhat capable of ripping it out of himself and throwing it at what was an extremely contrived oasis mirage, consisting entirely of a shoddy sign with the words 'Not Here' scrawled across it.

Ignoring the victory squeal of "Freee!" that his amputated appendix appeared to cry out during its sailing arc through the air, he continued his trek through the desert and straight to the cornucopia of glass and wire that encased Old Francisco.

Certainly, had any humans survived to see its erection, a few might have out-right died anyway from the very sight of what was once their worldly marvel. The outside of the micro-city took up only the space between the outer bridge arches, forming a dome that pierced the muck of water beneath it. Colour had long since faded from the streets of San Francisco, but the chronicle had an almost incandescent glow, something that could be put down to a severely failed Christmas lighting experiment from a while back, presumably before the creative bots were murdered.

The entrance stood proud; it was programmed that way when it used to run things at JC Penny, and right now it had to smell the daffodils for roses, or risk losing its own place in the world. In front further still, stood two stout guards, constructs you'd have hardly seen outside the military, brandishing copper-wire pikes that, even at risk of being crushed from a good sneeze, denoted some level of status.

"Hakt! Er, Halt!" A synchronised error that only confirmed their military origins. The leftmost guard pointed to a small, self-written 'Inspector' label as he approached Modbot confidently. "Now here see here, me and mine colleague there have to be making sure you are's who you says you are's before we lets you through! Can't have any *humans* coming in and mucking up the plac—"

The rightmost guard began almost immediately cowering, spinning, and rather loudly exclaiming, "Humans?!" before being hard-reset by a copper-wire pike to an overused side socket.

"Sees, me friend here's got the right idea; they're tricky business. So I look at you and I say… you're a penguin, what do you say?"

Modbot, not giving two shits in a shitter, offered little resistance, "I'm a penguin. Quack."

"It's a bloody penguin!" said the questioning guard in shock. "Well, go right aheads then, Sir Penguin, you let us know if you see any primates about you now!" He then hard reset himself in much the same way he had done to his colleague moments ago.

The door cracked open, muffling at a presumably inaudible volume, "A penguin? They're the worst, window shoppers without the windows." Modbot wasn't too perturbed by the whole penguin affair; he was simply trying to regain some sense of routine in a world that could not have further abandoned it.

It was at that moment he too heard the sky break as the gentle pitter patter of death danced around him.

Human - Folly

Two steps forward, one thousand back.

Tinker the digital and mangle the analogue, I struggle while others simply wait.

I won't let her lose herself, even if I'm worn to bones and ash, her light is more important.

Blinding.

But without sight, I at least not need see the day we part ways.

Chapter Eight - Metallurgy

Not quite accustomed to the idea of being shredded apart by the environment, you'd be hard pressed to blame either character for having second thoughts regarding this particular journey. You'd be especially hard pressed, because they didn't. Each having their own goal of such worth that even fate struggled at times to keep up appearances, cautiously reminding itself that if it wasn't menacing enough we might just get a chapter without melodramatic undertones for once.

Hours had passed since Usu suffered the most abusive medical care he could imagine, and he now found himself resting against Rain's stomach as she slept. She held her arms across her raised knees and her head limp upon them as if she was further sheltering Usu from whatever cards this frightening world still withheld.

The weather calmed as weathers oft tend to do, given enough time and paragraphs, of course. Rain awoke but pretended rather poorly not to have done so, if only to justify the mortal-coil bending squeeze she gave Usu before opening her eyes proper and letting out an exaggerated yawn. Her wounds were long gone, Usu had watched as each one slowly filled with a white paste, only to vanish in seconds. Rain seemed entirely oblivious to this, her concern waxed only to how good of a stitching job she'd managed. Dangling Usu from one arm and spinning him around to confirm a job well done, she proudly roared in a somewhat tactless expression of self-satisfaction, "Good as old!"

She stood and, with Usu still dangling upside down, carefully opened up their crumpled map. After spinning it enough degrees to make even the most stalwart protractor blush, she handed it to Usu for a rather dizzy deciphering. Being capable of the ancient art of telling upside down from not upside down, it didn't take all that much for him to point out where he estimated they were and, more importantly, where they needed to go. Probably.

"Rojah!" Following with a salute faster than adjectives could be bothered with, Rain tucked her fishing pole back in—Usu entwined once more—before taking a starting position you'd sooner see from a bobcat than an Olympian. The speed of her launch would scoff at both, however, allowing no time for dust to settle before leaving Lake Tahoe and the nightmare it bore far, far behind.

Some distance away, two fine and literal examples of shock therapy stood guard outside the very bastion of their kind which they had sworn to protect. At least they thought they had sworn to protect it, neither really remembered much; most of their usable memory appeared dedicated to some sort of penguin related trauma. A trauma soon to be far out-done by an encroaching blur.

Synthetic hair fluttered wildly, a wide smile began to reflect, and the very ground before the pair appeared to cry out as she landed, cracking asphalt with little regard. Steam still freshly wisping from her bare feet and a trail of ash thick in her wake, the rather human-looking girl stretched out her joints, leaned backward and declared victoriously, "Rain got faster!"

Military-grade robots had never known for their intellect, adaptability, or lack of masochistic tendencies, but they were pretty well known for thinking everything was going to kill them, which made them vigilant guardians during the brief moments they faked lucidity. "It's, it's," began the right-most of the pair before the left-most said, "No, no, don't you says it! Don't I says it either! A bloody huma—" an outburst cut short by a simultaneous, and perhaps instinctively by this point, copper-wire pike to each other's hard reset buttons. Now grounded—in more ways than one if puns be forgiven—the arguably saner of the pair struggled to his feet, neatly adjusted his 'Inspector' tag and maintained enough false poise to say, "Rights, passport then. Chop chop."

Rain, wise in the ways of the world as she clearly wasn't, responded profoundly, "Passport? Rain is Rain, not passport! Pfff."

Confounded by an intelligence perhaps parallel to his own, the inspector continued. "Now nows, look, I suppose I'd best explains. Firstly, me here is Inspector Cog." He made sure to puff out the part of his chest with the label, hoping none would see the words 'Janitor' scratched over ever so feverishly. "And that there is me sub-inspector, Wheel." A serious look overtook his already permanently serious façade, as he leaned in to say, "I know, I knows, but we'll have none of that silly punfoolery here! No jokes about WheelCog or the likes!"

Perhaps even more lost now than she was before, Rain found little to say and was rather haphazardly spinning Usu by his ears while Cog continued, seemingly unburdened by reality. "Nows! What I was going to have saids earlier was about your passport, you see." His eyes squinted ever so slightly. "Your kind—"

He was interrupted by Rain's logic circuits actually functioning, in a manner of speaking. "Rain is kind? Of course, Rain is kind! Meanies are boo."

Shaking his head, Cog tried again. "No, no, you… you know… the word we's can't have saids but did almost say," Wheel began screaming from the ground behind them, a small siren prematurely peeking from the tip of his head, "You don't mean hu—"

"No Noes! Yous don't says it!" Facing Rain again, "F-Fine we says you're something else, you're a… can you be a flamingo? We han't got one of those prissy buggers around. Go on 'en, make a flamingo noise!"

Challenged by the challenged, Rain searched her centuries of experience, her wealth of knowledge, and her stuffed rabbit cohort that was desperately trying to explain things to her through excessive sweating and arm waving. Somewhere deep, deep down, and then marginally deeper still, she found the answer, the answer to everything, but she sneezed and dropped that bit so she picked up the one next to it instead and confidently onomatopoeiad, "Meow?"

"It's a cat! It's a cat sir Cog, sir! It's come to eat the pengui—" Was as far as the hysterical Wheel got before being interrupted by a minor stab-induced electrical seizure. "Yes, you's no flamingo, definitely a cat. We's usually only let the birdses in but, I don't think poor Wheel can take many more stabs today. So against me better juryment, you're cleared Miss Cat! Just… don't eat all the birds now and do watch out for the primates, you never know when one could sneak by here when I'm not looking!" Cog said in a hushed voice, perhaps to keep his partner from undue distress, or perhaps just for dramatic purposes; no one cared enough to write another poorly comma'd sentence about it. Though, one could suppose the door cared, and probably would have commented too, if a rather disgruntled penguin had not ripped out any speaker related devices the night before in a perfectly calm rage-fueled moment of destructive euphoria. Instead, the door could do little to resist, even verbally. The once prized people appraiser that saw JC Penny reach new heights of personal degradation now silently opened its way for a little girl, her stuffed rabbit, and a fishing pole who soon blurred into the cityscape before them.

This particular chronicle, Old Francisco, was considered a marvel even among robots specifically engineered to be obsessively cynical in an attempt at solving the mass critic-shortage that sneaked up on the 22nd century. 'Sneaked' being your narrator's euphemism for the part where they were all killed. Book critics were first, you remember that now.

Still, inappropriate revelations about career tracks ignored, the city was indeed a sight to behold. None of that flying car nonsense you've mucked about with in your head. For all the wire, degrading neon tubes, and fiber the city felt motionless, a silence made eerie by visuals that did little to justify it. The fully spherical structure had strut upon strut of transparent solar paneling inside, a sight marred only by the bare connecting wires sapping life from each one. At its base, the sphere barely pierced what was now a truly dead sea, cycling water from it to cool itself.

Rain and Usu stood on a thick glass walkway, caught between each extreme and a very friendly looking sign that insisted they both 'Sod off'. Then, just as Rain found herself mumbling the words aloud, the silence broke. Awakening from its daily slumber, the chronicle sprung to life and the exceptionally friendly sign swiveled around to be replaced with a far shinier one bearing a far gentler (if generic) banner, 'Welcome'. Robotic birds began to sing from suspended power cables while robotic hillbillies began to shoot at them from shanty rooftops, and in a determined response robotic Europeans felt mild discomfort at the display.

They stood before the hawkers market which, due to trigger-happy hillbillies, had long since done away with any pun related associations to the word hawk. Instead, ancient programming kept them bartering to any prey that would enter their sights, the less self-aware would do so for merchant masters that had long since faded past even the concept of bone meal. Yet, unlike most days which they would spend bartering their own essential parts away to each other, this day new prey *had* actually wandered into their sights.

Amidst the buildings, coloured and crooked in homage to their namesake, swarms of hagglers approached, merciless in their mercantile ways. They offered Rain dolls, makeup, and hair accessories. They offered Usu a box he'd fit in with a low price-tag on it. They were a crafty lot. They were also there at the worst possible time: The time when Rain's time stopped. She froze again like so many times before, and Usu could only try and keep the scavengers at bay until one noticed what had happened to her. Suddenly, signals spread like wildfire, and dread gripped each one of them as they backed away silently, too frightened to even break eye contact, as if for the first time they were staring down their own demise in this world flooded with immortality. It mattered little.

All beings cowered under death.

Android - The First Day

I met a total weirdo Diary! I mean okay, okay, he saved me and stuff, after I crawled in the garbage shoot to get away from those meanies, but he was all "Bssshwing" and "Shwwaaaggh" cutting me down and then he was actually disappointed I was awake! So boo!

But… there's something there, something that feels important.

It felt like if I didn't follow him, I'd never follow anyone again.

Chapter Nine - Crumpets

If you've been trying to link chapter titles to chapter content this far along, you've been trying longer than your own narrator. Although, perhaps crumpets are indeed the perfect metaphor for how Rain's body froze in motion, assuming you've frozen the crumpets, which will taste terrible when you reheat them. You're an odd one, I'll give you that, but what you won't be given is any more crumpets, lest you freeze them like the confectionery tyrant we both now know you to be.

Even fourth walls were looking sturdier than our heroine right now; her arms limp and her upper half concaving. Usu was struggling just to keep her standing, a struggle he'd fought this far for, and a struggle he'd be willing to fight as far for as long as need be. He would not let her get hurt, he would not let her fall, and somewhere in the back of his mind a voice much like his own echoed that he would not fail her, not again. Never again.

Right about now, you'd expect some sort of cliché rescue scene; maybe Modbot would come in from a random corner of the sphere and merrily un-muck-up things. He wouldn't though; he was preoccupied with equally personal matters. Yet, in haste not to disappoint you, the dear valued reader, there was a figure speeding toward them across each rooftop, feet flinging tiles as if they were confetti. This figure landed next to Usu and picked Rain up in a way Usu had long wished he had the might to do himself. It was a slender, feminine figure, obvious even through the black rags she had cloaked all but her eyes with, but she was no android. A darker shade of silver took the place of her skin, and her every movement seemed like clockwork. She looked Usu in the eyes, tied his arms around her neck and whispered, "Hold on tight, knots aren't exactly my specialty," before running up the side of the nearest building, a foot casually decapitating a wild hillbilly bot in process.

By now, Usu was rather accustomed to situations

one should generally avoid altogether, especially ones involving dangerous women flinging him about at high speeds. Given his earlier experience with Rain, you could say this was an almost calming 300mph stroll across perfectly agreeable rooftops. He found little fear to settle his confusion, and thus began nudging his kidnapper for answers. Little did he notice that she was already engaged in some primitive form of mono-synchronistic dialogue, or at least that's what we'll call her muttering repeated curse words under her—albeit artificial—breathe. Indeed the stream of endlessly repeating 'Shit!' whilst speeding along, made her slightly more intimidating, but Usu nudged on despite her fascination with fecal matter.

"Shitbeard is going to wet himself over thi—Oh, uhm, alright back there? I'm sure you're all full of questions dear, but let's save those for the landing alright? Don't worry, if anyone can dissassem—er, help her, it's where we're going!" she said before immediately dulling her eyes to a half-gaze and returning to her rather abusive rattling.

It occurred to Usu just then that, despite memories of Rain and of his other-self beginning to make him whole, he'd not heard any decent swearing until that moment. Rain would probably start a jar if anyone did it and use the funds to buy a bigger jar, eventually forgetting her purpose in life and seeking the path of ultimate jar transcendence instead. While Modbot, well, he was sure he'd cursed a few hundred or so times, but he was so British about it that he didn't even take notice, contrary to this 'girl' and her sweet American voice degrading into something verbally pungent enough to raise a middle-school hall monitor's wrath and ire. Thankfully, all of those were also rather somewhat completely dead.

The scenery, verbally diluted by everything being covered in audible shit, was rather astonishing. It seemed that where they came to was but the proverbial rabbit-hole to this vibrant wonderland. Districts divided areas with massive concrete and wire walls, thick metal gates being the official links between each one. He spotted dozens, from vertical residential areas to the hollow shells of industrial plants; it seemed almost as if they had made this land ripe with the memory of the long-gone race that created them. Was it an homage? Or a hope, a strange twisted hope from a stranger still land?

Casino's in one corner, patrons coming out with fewer limbs than they went in with, contrasted starkly with the Marina in the other end. It seemed to send orbs out through the bottom of the city into the water below, shooting them with such force that even their direction could be little more than a guess. What was at least slightly alarming was that none ever seemed to come back up, more reminiscent of an escape pod than a transportation system. The idea of being hurled into the dead ocean didn't seem appetising to him either way though. Usu always had an innate fear of whales and presumed dead ones would be all the more terror-worthy.

Speaking of terror-worthy, Usu, Rain, and the mysterious assailant were about to land, it seemed. She'd moved nimbly enough to satiate even the most hardcore parkour fetishist, leaping from rooftop to boundary, detachable head to asphalt and finally down a time-worn chute. The fall wasn't long, eight maybe nine seconds, but enough for him to hear a very familiar voice, disgruntled to say the least protesting, "Blimey! Look, all I want is for you and your sharp bits there to come tally-ho and right chop this door voice modulator off of what may or may not be my crotch." Countered by a hoarse brazen voice, with just enough Scottish in it to make you feel sexually displaced at any given moment, "I am lookin' laddy, 'n whit I'm seein' is ye wanting tae just separate 'hings again. Just choap it aff aye? Is easy aye? Just pretend it wasn't even thar aye?! Och, ah know yer kind."

Volatile as things may have been, the sudden landing into the midst of a robo-anatomical bickering match actually proved a positive thing.

The duo's mysterious abductor landed in a small crater that barely broke the panorama of steel tiles and busted VCR machines, a comfortable fit for few others. Looking up, she couldn't withhold her excitement and ran forward yelling, "Shitbea—Dad!" before hugging the most bizarre creature Usu had seen yet.

To only mildly disappoint your descriptive expectations, allow your narrator to elaborate: What he saw was clearly mechanical and clearly robotic, like everything he'd seen thus far, but was first and foremost hanging upside down from a rooftop he wished was further and further away. Masculine in features, a strong jaw, square eyes, and a peculiar beard made from what presumably was a sea of left-over arms dangling about. Not to be outdone, the rest of him was dangling about as well; his body began normal enough, shoulders, a neck. It even had good torso potential! Unfortunately, the reality was an arachnid-like bulbous exterior with half a dozen legs on each side, strange work tools welded into most of them. His powers of deduction having grown exponentially since the whole adventure had begun, Usu didn't take long to grasp this was the oh-so-elegantly proclaimed 'Shitbeard'.

"Och, we're 'n polite mode are we? Mist be fer th' find. What's this noo? Ah, haven't seen one o' these in weel... in ever!" said the supposedly fecal-bearded mystery as he kicked himself off the wall and toward Rain and Usu. Purely cosmetic defensive instincts as they may have been, Usu's attempt to safeguard Rain was met with a dual surprise, both at the owner of the familiar voice being Modbot and that he was actually happy to see them.

"Usu! Weather channel! Oh, I missed you both like Thatcher missed her penis whenever they got around to removing it. Now wait... the lass, Rain, I do recall her being a might more chipper than limp and stony eyed." Though he was possibly just as pleasantly surprised for the first time in his life, the whole limp, near-death business put a bit of a damper on things. Just when he was thinking how he could get Usu to explain what had transpired, his crotch—now plus one module—insisted, "Quickly, explain through interpretive terror dance!" before Modbot could smack it into submission. "Ah, this, this is well, the door and, we disagreed and, well I'm just trying to get this blathering blout to chop the bugger off actually. I hear he does things like that, probably could help the girl too, or just yell at her for asking; seems best at that last bit actually." While not exactly the greatest news, it did calm Usu down a fair deal and allow for Rain to be peeked at properly without him lunglessly hyperventilating.

"Laddie, dae ye even know whit this 'ere lassie is?" Stroking his beard as elegantly as one could stroke a 2-foot long dangling set of limbs hanging off of a chin, Shitbeard continued. "Ah rate ye dinnae even know whit ye yerself are, eh?"

Usu could do little to hide his growing insecurities over his own identity, which memories were his, and why he was here in the first place.

Rain's downfall had taken precedence in his mind, ignoring the questions that had been gnawing away at him from the inside out. He shook his head, averting his gaze in the process. "Ha, that's fin'. Ah don't ken whit in th' hells ye are either, laddie! All ah know is these 'ere eyes," he flipped fancifully through several settings on his lensed orbs. "Nae a thing they ain't able tae see, 'n in ye? Not a single movin' pairt, just fluffy stuffin'. Yit ye shift aboot mair than me own daughter when you're popp'n a fuss!"

He let out an overdrawn synthetic sigh, making sure to coat Modbot in most of the passing smog before continuing. "The lass, well, she's special too, but naught 'n a good way lad. Androids like her, they were all hunt'd down fer fear, fear they might become the new humanitae. But it's worse in this case; she mighta' avoided the grubbies, but the damn girl went and set off her killswitch." Now even Shitbeard averted his gaze, he'd done this for a long, long time, and giving bad news never got easy.

Modbot, rather helpful as he was very occasionally known to be, immediately knew both the terror of what this meant and that Usu would need a proper explanation. "Blue-arsed flies, I wish I could say he was lying, but a killswitch is our worst fear Fluffpuff. You know how we don't age, or even decay much because even rust isn't alive right?" Usu worryingly nodded, one eye focused in each direction. "Well, humans, arses as they were and all, decided it would only be right and proper to stop us from making more of ourselves. You know, so we couldn't make an evil robot army and kill them, instead of them suffocating one by one in their colonies or being poisoned by acid rain. No, no. Robot zombie armies were *clearly* the bigger danger there. So whatever tosser was in charge at the time thought it would be clever to set us to shut down if we ever saw any robotic schematics. For most of us, that would mean a short-term memory wipe and a good poke to get back on, but for androids? They were scared bridges to britches of the buggers, so their killswitch it... it causes them to lose *all* their memories and eventually disassemble entirely. She... must have seen one somewhere. Blight, the fact that it hasn't taken her fully yet is a miracle in its own way."

Spreading a smoggy sigh purposdentally across Modbot once again, our more medically inclined ally chimed back in. "Aye, haggisballs thar speaks truth laddie. Th' lassie won make it, hells, only reason ah kin repair others is a faulty switch 'n meself. Ah kin wake her up wance, bit th' next time sh' freezes, she won' be wak'n up again. Ah kin promise ye that either wey." Reluctantly, Usu agreed; Rain needed to know, she needed to decide her fate, or find some way—trifle or not—to fight it.

Fingers tingled, eyes were wet, and one little girl woke up from one nightmare into another.

Android - The Next Day

He let me in, I didn't think he would, not like sleeping against his only window was that bad, but it's… nicer inside. His name is Snow, he got pretty upset when I kept calling him wafflehair boy, but I thought it was waaay cuter!

I never believed in names Diary, but he says they're important, I don't know if I want one… but can I call you Dee?

It's small inside, but it feels warm and he even lets me use a spare room! Though, whenever I ask who it belonged to he gets sad, but one time he smiled instead and said, "It belongs to you now."

Can things like me have homes Dee?

Chapter Ten - Myyrth

You'd think making something able to weep profusely might be a low-priority feature, but you've read this far so it would be wise not to put much faith in what you think. Instead, the cruel reality drenched Usu's paws once more, as he desperately tried to catch her tears, perhaps fearing that each and every one was a piece of her, a piece he couldn't do without.

At that moment, even Rain wished she didn't retain her senses during her blackouts. She had heard every word, and every part of her body reverberated the truth in them. Minutes of sniffling (and rather pointless paw swiping) passed until she could move freely, and through every ache she pulled Usu close, hugging him tightly before saying, "I'm, I'm sorry Snow. I'm sorry for everything. I'm even sorry I'm crying, silly right?" She pressed her forehead to his and forced a smile across her drenched face.

Manchester, as the disturbingly multi-legged mechanic turned out to be named after proper introductions were handled, was stroking his limb-beard at the sight, occasionally tickling himself into an embarrassed giggle before regaining composure. Then, when he felt he'd probably pass out from the strangling hug his daughter was still curiously rather intent on doing to him, he decided to speak up. "Now now lass, wipe yer sprockets 'n polish yer nugge—oh right, ye don't have those be'n a lass 'n all. What aye meant t'say is, I n'er said there wan't a way to save ye, or, at least try." Pulling himself back into the upper reaches of the room, he proceeded to scratch a strange pattern in a tile, moments later a massive terminal lowered and his endless stream of chin-arms sprung to life, weaving a marvelous tapestry of taps across it. The screen changed a multitude of times, reflecting across his metallic sheen before settling on a single image, casting a blue hue across the room. He faced the pair again, lunging to sexual harassment distance in a heartbeat before finally revealing his cards. "Now, tis true that yer 'n trouble lass, but trouble's me middle hand! Somewhere 'n there at least." Rain looked up with half-open eyes, trying her best to stop each tear before it began as he continued. "But there's a way, or half a way at least I'd wager. Yer schematics, likes o' which I've naer seen, could be enough fer me to help ye. Better yet, they're so rare y'd end up paying fer the help at the same time lass!"

"Rain can… can stay with Snow?" she managed before taking one last deep, hopeful sniff.

"Snew? The rabbit? Aye, if you kin get yer soul-scribbles I'll do wha' I can. Ye have me word, an'… an' me daughter! Ye kin borrow her fer a bit, maybe teach her some manners?" He was interrupted with a barely feminine growl dangling from what could possibly be called his neck.

"The hell you mean *manners*? Shitbeard, I swear if I eventually find the washer that connects your ass to your fac—"

A rather terrified look crossed Manchester's

brow as he interjected, "S-She's a sweet lass! Charming! Best thing I e'er made!"

Seemingly calmed by a fair degree or two, the still-cloaked and apparently personality disorder-stricken daughter swiveled onto one hand and dropped directly in front of Usu. "Yeah so, we already met and all, but the name is Mercury. Dad over there is probably wanting to send us to what you see on that screen there. It's the place where they developed your girl. Bit of a suicide trip, he's been trying to send me there alone for years now. Claims it's half the reason he built me without a killswitch in the first place." Her eyes, which were startlingly human-like along with being the only part clearly exposed from her cloak, showed equal parts disinterest, disappointment, and empathy. "But hey, it's fine, I shut off the power relays connecting him to the solar panel systems earlier, so if we don't make it back he'll die too!" she said while scruffing up Rain's hair in an unusual attempt to lighten the mood.

Laughing in an uneasy terror as his arms tried to reach behind him to confirm her threat, Manchester briefed them in the most long-winded way one could. "Ye see the photo there laddie? That'd be the lab, more than half a millennium in disuse, bit ye kin bet yerself a piece o' stuffin' that the data ye want is 'n it! Only trouble is what ye see around it there, all tha' silly water nonsense ye know. Tis a wee bit… uncooperative." As he said this, Usu, despite his lack of formal sign language training, was rather sure he saw one of the chin-hands mimic a slit throat and another slap an invisible knee in laughter.

Encouraging.

"The Hatchery, as it was called in its day, was wee more than an electronic part parade tae the public, but I'd bet mah independence the lassie there wasn't just born there, she wis conceived." Lurching ever closer with each sentence. "Anything ye fin' there, be it designs or pieces o' her kin, could save her."

Silently observing until then, Modbot spoke up. "I'll go with you Bunbun. I mean, I've got nothing better to do, and Blimey that place is probably in need of a serious cleaning!" he proclaimed while shying away from outright admittance, but edging close enough to impress his dangling nemesis, who then promptly chopped off the extra attachment from his crotch with a swift stroke from a random arm.

"Bastards 'll probablae need me t'fix the door eventually anywae." Manchester thereby unburdened Modbot for whatever lay in wait, or perhaps just took the opportunity to chop his not-so-proverbial knob off. Probably the latter.

Now knobless, Modbot swung Usu around his back so he sat rather snugly between his incineration module and the rest of himself. Mercury was already piggybacking Rain, who was still waning her way out of grand sobbetry, when she gave Usu the sort of wink only someone who has kidnapped you and tried to sell of your body parts can give, and she gave it well. Winks be done, she left little time to waste, leaping out of what was presumably once upon a time a one-way entrance. By the time Modbot had used his extensive set of transversal skills to climb the ladder out, barely an echo could be seen or heard of them, already atop a great boundary and tearing away at any form of flooring that happened to be cursed enough to lay in Mercury's path.

Usu was attempting to shake the gobsmacked Modbot into some sort of similar action but the cleaning robot's rather appropriate response was, "Now, during our wonderful time of almost dying together ad nauseam, do you recall me ever leaping anything higher than myself? Because I'll be snogfairied if we're going that way, and trust me, I'm pretty sure neither of us wants to be snogfairied." Left at a loss for words, let alone the ability to say them, Usu couldn't put up much more resistance in earnest. "Good! Then we'll be heading to the docks like gentlemen! That is: Through a dozen doors, about three hills and then I think we can just roll downwards until we hit something. I have it on pretty good authority it's how people used get around this area, plus or minus a few bits of genitalia, of course."

Modbot wasn't kidding. About an hour of walking, another of complaining about the overwhelming amount of simulated Coffee shops, and another chasing down a pink piñata that had survived a fair deal better than the species that made it, they finally arrived, smashing Usu-first into a port barricade. Usu probably should have become more suspicious when Modbot tied him to his face as a 'precaution', though an accurate one it had been. Rain was there to offer him the same comfort he'd given her not so long ago through a hug that would make anyone grateful to lack bone structure while gleefully spinning him around as if the encroaching nightmare was but a fleeting dream.

"Snooow! Slow Snow! But still Snow!" She looked off to the side in Mercury's direction with a mighty pout. "Pillow-case lady wouldn't let me go find you, says I can't exert myself right now, but Pillow-cases aren't even supposed to talk!" said the oblivious girl to the stuffed rabbit before her.

Mercury was leaning against a railing in casual annoyance, obviously having expected some sort of competition from Modbot, who was rather unwisely attempting his first conversation with her. "So! You were actually built by that geezer? You're… rather young then, I take it? Never around for the humans? Oh, you didn't miss much, too little air for them to even scream properly in the end, which made cleaning up after them a mite bit easier, I'll have you know!" Laughing awkwardly to himself, he subtly squashed the remnants of a completely irrelevant piñata into his incinerator.

Mercury scowled, or was constipated, things are hard to judge through an eye slit. "Manchester, yeah, he built me. I'm his 'shining star of success', considering the only other things he built are those hillbillies that pop up around the place. He's been trying to kill me for years now though, or was that what I've been doing? Details. But hey, we haven't exactly got all day if we want to get there." She tucked a piece of silver hair back into her head wrap while briefly making eye-contact with what was beginning to resemble a sunset on prescription anthrax.

She'd long since prepared for the departure, the strangely unnatural pier beside her was aloft with water, much like the rest of the city's bottom level. Next to Mercury bobbed a large transparent yet thick and slimy ball with one large hole atop for entrance, an entrance she used rather abruptly when she dropped Rain, Usu, Modbot and her rather brash self through all at once. She traced her fingers around the edges of the hole, which sealed itself instantly and began shedding thicker and thicker slime until their slow descent into purgatory began.

Android - The Day Forgotten

I messed up Dee. I messed up really, really bad.

Snow, he… he kept telling me not to go into his workshop, but you kinda have to when someone says that right? It was amazing at first, all these bits and pieces of shinies he was taking apart to make the little woof-woofs and meows he sells, they were all sooo cute! But I wasn't supposed to be there… I was rolling and playing before some weird papers with scribbles fell on me, and when I looked at them something happened.

Something inside me burst into a million pieces and I couldn't move until Snow found me. I've never seen him cry Dee, but it's all he could do. He never shouted at me or told me I was bad, he just kept hugging me and saying sorry.

One of those fragile pieces got much, much bigger that day.

Chapter Eleven - Sanguine

Machinations never did quite find the same appreciation for water humans were so well known for, probably because it could kill them, but at least partially because its very nature went against their own. The tide waxes and wanes, the ocean swells, and once upon a time even birthed life. The same life that went on to make them. To all but a few, thoughts of becoming a creator were horror stories of wiped memories and fragmented thoughts. As free as they were, they remained slaves to programming, dwelling on the devil in their data and fearing the excel spreadsheet that hides under their beds.

For the few that faced demons greater still, however, it was an escape. Ironic as the steel it was built upon then, that the chronicle of Old Francisco, born from the structure once called 'Suicide Bridge', would continue to hold onto death; living patrons be damned. Dozens every day, twofold by night. The number rose as the years did, and soon bloomed a deadly reputation to match. Those who could not take the world as it was, those who were lost without their masters, and those who had forgotten them completely. All manners entered the peaceful marina, and only one rather rude one expected to return.

If forced to pick sides, Mercury would sooner turn to genocide than suicide. She entered this watery coffin with more than a mere plan up her jumble of cloth. She'd get to the underwater laboratory, called 'The Hatchery' during its better years, and 'Holy Shit' during the present, at least by the one person aboard who actually knew where it was. Several miles west and many more down, the ruins stood brightly lit, beckoning from a sea floor awash with well-whittled bones.

Yet, they faced the initial problem of actually moving in a direction other than down, a problem becoming more and more pressing as Rain insisted she could probably have a quick lick outside the bubble and be fine. Slightly wiser in the ways of the world, Modbot did what he could to convince her otherwise. Indeed, no easy task.

Mercury, in the meantime, gently pierced the outer lining with a small rectangular device that whirred to life the instant it felt the cold embrace surrounding them.

Despite a round of shock and confusion, she hushed the group and watched the device with a nervous intensity. Finally, a stream of energy shot out from it with the kind of force that can call out a jet engine as limp and in need of erectile assistance. They had covered a tremendous distance before a crack was heard and the device shattered completely. Mercury explained the situation to the others. "We should be directly above it now, I've got one more of those but, well, best we save that for making our trip back a tad less of a crotch shot." Now, they knew, came the somewhat less pleasant part.

The 'less pleasant part' was that, by design, the

bubbles based their physical buoyancy on the mood of the respective suicidee. Should they truly wish to end it all, sinking was inevitable, but second thoughts or that fiendish thing we call hope, well, then it would rise to the surface and pop, giving them a few precious moments of life's blissful struggle before promptly drowning to death. This did pose a minor problem, in thanks to Usu's stalwart nature and Rain's love of everything, which were surely flight risks. However, they were in luck having chosen a prototype model with a very special feature to ensure automated sinking. A large portion of the vessel changed before Usu's eyes, transparency was replaced by opaqueness. It began flickering, and static fumbled like maggots playing tennis for a bit before a human appeared, long blond hair, a muscular frame, standing before an anesthetized crowd.

That moment, and several hundred thereafter, they would learn true terror, true fear, and true disdain as they were forced to listen a cacophony of screams and moaning playing over a video recording of Michael Bolton live in concert and on repeat. Unfortunately, all of the overdubbed shrieks and death rattles could do little to drown out his Dolby digitally enhanced voice.

They sank, and sank further still until, dazed and confused, without mental mettle or hope in heart they were sucked down within a tunnel and emerged into the dim light of salvation. The song stopped as each occupant crawled out onto the hangar's metal skirts. Even Mercury couldn't maintain her façade, throwing up some strange black bile away from the stumbling Usu and teary-eyed Rain, who could only mumble, "Why are there bad men like that Snow? W-Why must they hurt Rain?" with an innocent pained look that could almost put her dire future at second fiddle.

The loading bay they found themselves inside of was—perhaps evidenced by the suction tunnel—not one intended for humanoid entrance, and probably even less so for that of a stuffed rabbit. The room held barely enough solid steel ground for them to regain their not-so-proverbial bearings, most of it awash with a dense water that reeked with a promiscuous blend of antiseptics and iron. A far too familiar smell to Usu, from long-gone days when blood and metal held him firmly in their grip.

Yet, despite smells or horrendous transportation methods, the facility retained a pristine quality about itself. Not a light was broken nor a sign askew. Even the laughable idea of a pressurisation chamber held them for a few peaceful hours before Modbot accidentally ripped the door off whilst ever more accidentally having it hit the automated comm speaker. Means and methods behind them now, they were inside and well on their way to making some form of progress, that is until Usu's foot took yet another fateful step.

With one movement, a simple paranoid attempt to check around a corner before facing it, the very tile he stood upon began to emit light, spreading across the room like wildfire until, at it's climax, the light burst, giving way to darkness. Faint mumbles echoed across the hallways as faint, ghost-like holograms began trudging along in lab coats, some arguing, some laughing, some making dinner plans. It felt alive, as alive as anyone else there at least. But it remained only a memory, a fragment of time preserved for some unknown purpose. A fragment that pulled at something inside Usu, and twisted something inside Rain. There was great sadness here, and it resonated deeply within both of them, so much so that their eyes didn't even need to meet to know the other felt it too. This was a rather good thing, because Usu was, at the time, being held against Rain's stomach upside down, a truly awkward position for eye contact.

Mercury was first to break the air. "Right, I know, spooky weird shit, but unless you want that princess here as a doorstop, we've got to spend more time moving and less gawking."

Rain, worried far more for how Usu would take such a reality than she would, faced Mercury, squinted up into her eyes, slammed both her legs together and her free arm against her forehead. "Yes sir, Lady sir!" She proclaimed before being gone in a heartbeat. The trail of ground debris among the digital sheen wrote her path rather clearly and didn't do the holograms passing over it much good either.

"Riiight, so they've gone that way, what say we go the opposite?" Mercury put forth in a rather meager attempt to maintain a façade of complete calm.

Modbot had his doubts, however. "Wait lass, you're saying the girl and rabbit will be fine alone? I doubt Usu could defeat a kitchen counter on a good day, and the girl, well– " He was interrupted by the first giggle Mercury may have had since her mechanical life began.

"Ha, I take it you haven't seen her in action then have you? How long would it take you to cross a state? A day?" Modbot nodded while trying incredibly hard not to think of Utah. "Well this girl? Minutes. I could see them approaching through the chronicle's glass, her speed alone broke what little air remains. I'd say she's probably the strongest here, narcolepsy aside. You, bum-chum, on the other hand probably need someone level headed around to stop you from mounting 'modules' to your... areas..."

Aghast, agape, and alliteratively abused, Modbot had little in the way of argument. Frankly speaking, he was just glad she didn't insist on calling him Haggisballs like her father.

The group's paths diverged, yet their wills aligned. Each pair sought out Rain's schematics, or at least those of an android like her. The Hatchery had born each and every android to ever walk the earth and there was, therefore, little doubt it held what they sought. Doubt, perhaps, at what good Modbot could do rummaging around while blindfolded to avoid his own kill-switch activating, but none regarding their prize.

Rain's blitzkrieg was finally halted by Usu's thirty-ninth tug on her hair; presumably attempts one through thirty-eight being sloppy pulls with little heart. This particular pull, however, was marvelous; it had firmness, grip, and just the right amount of yank to snap someone out of a self-induced flurry. They stopped just before a solid antiquated pressure door, it was built thick even for its kind and bore only the word 'Olive' neatly above a slit of blackened glass. The opening mechanism posed little trouble for Rain's strength, yet just before the final turn she found herself hesitant and overcome with a feeling of wrongness.

Perhaps it was this feeling that manifested behind her as a small voice yelled, "Stop!" There stood a flickering image of someone much like Rain, yet considerably younger. A girl of five or six, and while a hologram like the rest, she looked intently at them both. This one wasn't a mere memory; it was something else, something with a frighteningly strong will. She had tears in her eyes as both faced her, a small smile in response. "Th-Thank you. That place is bad," she said, pointing directly at the door. "It gave a lot, but took so much more. It isn't safe inside, but I… I know you need to go in. Just please be careful and…" Her image now barely holding the weight of light "...Promise you won't get angry." She then vanished completely. Usu searched the area where she appeared but found naught. Rain made the final turn of the wheel, clicking open with a slow hiss. Nothing scared her anymore, nothing but losing the one she loved. To save him the pain she once felt, she had to save herself. After all, he'd kept his part of a promise stronger than the very tapestry of life, she had only to keep hers.

Android - The Best Day

Someone is writing weird stuff in you Dee! They write a bit like me, but nuh-uh, I know my Dee back to front! Though, some of them are nice to read. I'd like to pretend me and Snow really did do some of the things written down.

So even if it's a lie, it's a nice one.

But you know what's even nicer?

We totally had a date, like grown-ups! I was all "Rain has present!" He was all glowing red and then he took me out to say thank you! He was a little mad at me for hurting my fingers so much knitting it for him, but that's just because Snow cares, Dee. Snow even sleeps with it by his pillow now! But he still notices when I try and sneak in, I'll have to make the next bunny waaay bigger.

If anything ever happened to me, you'd be there for him, right Dee?

Chapter Twelve - Dandruff

Harmony, while a fairly simple concept, exhibits a contrastingly complex execution. There is harmony in death, chaos in life, and in between both there's a considerable amount of scalp shedding. Still, at its prime, The Hatchery aimed to personify both harmony and creation, concepts its denizens could not truly fathom at the time. Creation is born from the very dissonance they saw themselves elevated above, yet even so, the hammer of history falls ever hardest on those who dare stand tall and defiant.

There were some, however, who would crawl through the very mud and muck of Genesis itself to see a small dream born. Amidst the drones of flesh and the flicker of liquid crystal, two women had worked tirelessly, very much aware of the doomed world lingering above, but unwavering all the same. They had lost someone even more precious than each other, and they would fight even their own sanity to bring them back.

Pustules of organic matter and yards of fiber optics had littered their lab; screams had become dull to both, a meager side effect when gathering parts. Their laboratory, long cut off by both rumours and steel plating, stood as a rotten core of an even more befouled fruit. Their actions cruel and deviant, but their motivations pure as any life they took. The section they laboured in was named 'Olive', and it was the very same one Rain and Usu found themselves entering.

Immediately, with little pause for puns, a dank, humid and dreadfully thick excuse for air burst past them. The pressure of the room had presumably not come to terms with the rest of the building, releasing itself as a pungent, sweaty haze that overrode most of their senses. Despite a complete absence of light, they took slow, blind steps inward, making sure to hold hands because it was only touch that they could trust at the moment. Touch did not lie as far as most senses go, but held itself as a rather blunt instrument for delivering the truth, ever more so when undesired. Unfortunately touch also included a soft squishing from beneath their footfalls. They continued, the squishes grew louder, and each could feel some form of liquid beginning to hit ankle depth.

You, being a seasoned reader, probably suspect that liquid to be blood. You also thought that last piece of cake wasn't going straight to your hips and we both know who was wrong there. It was oil. Mostly oil. Oil and blood, but we're really focusing on your failure here so keep your mind on the oil part.

Yet both failure and creepy squishy noises only serve to make some stronger. They continued, slowly encroaching on what must be the center, with Rain hoisting Usu to sit up around her shoulders as the viscous liquid reached bunny-hazardous heights. Then, with a graceful sort of clumsiness, Rain stumbled onto something, falling face-flat onto a cold, hard and somewhat unwelcoming granite slab.

"Booo!" echoed the room as she pulled herself up, Usu trying to help despite basic physics disagreeing with such an idea. Like so much in this building, their actions were not without consequence. Dripping sounds began as Rain managed to sit up, soon turning into a roaring downpour until, less than twenty seconds later, stopping completely. Time seemed to crack around them, and faster than either could comprehend, the room was lit with a dizzying brightness that poured forth from antique lamps in each corner. Below them the river of oil and blood became blatantly visible, only made gentle in comparison to the grafted flesh polyps they had evidently been stepping on. Neither fancied the idea of getting off that slab now, wondering if a few hundred more years might help all that icky nonsense dry up like a right mess should.

But there was little right in this space.

The scent of death had long permeated there,

perhaps a small consolation that they didn't know the smell from any other foul muck, yet it held no saving graces for the victims of the past. Victims who had been torn apart piece by piece, dematerialized and reconstituted without a passing sweat. The room had given birth to many, but torn apart scores more, all to appease the ambitions of the pair who had mastered this butchery. A pair who, through sheer force of digitized will, found themselves appearing before Usu just then.

Wailing, the likes of which a banshee might blush at, made the liquid ripple in response as two wisps of light took form. Each a young woman, one bespectacled while the other had presumably opted for contacts during her breathing years. They stared at each other for a good moment, something warm seemed to pass between them until they set their eyes on Rain. "Oh, dear Catherine, it's one of the failures again," said the bespectacled hologram to her partner who was frisking her own digitized hair in discomfort.

"No, no, Catherine darling, we made sure to dispose of all of those, remember? This surely can't be one of ou—" She leaned in and squinted her eyes before letting out a shrill squeak. "Number Eight! Why it *is* Number Eight! Remember her? Oh, she was a tricky one my love, but a failure nonetheless."

The two morally impaired and apparently identically named holograms persisted at each other. "I'm sure we put her in the disposal section like the rest, quite a shame, she took *so* many parts, after all. Not sure how she survived, not for much longer though, her switch has been triggered. Hmm, why did we put those in them again?"

Glasses Catherine checked her lab-coat for any digitized faults before bringing her attention back. "Mutiny darling, mutiny! The administrators were all fine and dandy sending us meat to work with, but heaven forbid the children learn how to make each other! Well, a bit late for that I suppose."

Equally startled by the disturbingly illuminating situation, Usu and Rain peered back ever so quizzically until Rain let slip, "Failure? Number Eight? Pfft, Rain is Rain!" A proud statement made all the more firm by Usu folding his arms and crossing his brow as she said it. It had impact, it had emotion, and it had numerous other things the lab fiends before them had struggled to understand even in life.

Swiftly an exchange passed between them once more. "She's been named!" "She thinks she has a name!" "Only dear Olive deserved a name, silly thing." "She's certainly no Olive." "Neither were numbers nine through four hundred though, a shame really."

Rain, ever more flummoxed by their use of vocabulary and vague story scraps let out her loudest "Booo!" to try and gain attention, turning to Usu and declaring, "Rain doesn't want help from crazy ladies! Can we go Snow?"

"She's talking to the doll?" "The doll is moving darling." "So it is! Hmm, odd that." "Oh very." "Do you suppose we should show her how we made her?" "For proof or giggles?" "Both, as always!" A sweet glare shot between each of them, veiling a far more sinister intent. Before Rain or Usu could get off the slab, a screen entered their vision, the display lighting up one liquid crystal at a time until something altogether unimaginable began playing. Granted, their most recent experience with digital displays had been rather nightmarish so they both elicited immediate fear, pursuing the contents with one apprehensive eye each.

Before them, they saw what looked like the room they now occupied with a pristine sheen far removed from its present condition. Tiles of white were baked into every corner, and the slab they now rested on was of similar colour. Yet as it played, the image skipped, skipping again thrice more until steadying on the same scene but with a middle-aged man strapped to the slab, both Catherines dancing to a distant piano as he screamed in agony. He began frothing at the mouth as his body thrashed against the restraints until Glasses-Catherine simply leant backward in her waltz, effortlessly injecting him in the neck. The piano grew louder, the screen flashed again nearly a dozen times, yet in one brief heartbeat Usu was sure he saw what became of that man, pieces of him lined neatly across the slab, every limb scrutinized.

But that was not meant to be seen, instead the scene settled on two young girls squeezed down to fit the same table brace. A cybernetic limb on each, one an arm another a leg, but neither seemed to be conscious as the dance continued around them. The piano did not stop, but their dance did. Seconds later both could be seen lifting up each arm, measuring them, comparing them, counting the parts in their cybernetic attachments. Crows pecking at tied prey, made only truer still when the entire screen was coated in a dark brown colour edging on red. Images quickly flickered forward once again.

Then, as if to show the secret behind a magic trick, there were no more illusions. The image was clear, walls had been speckled, floors coated, and two dancing mistresses of the carrion could be seen spinning, cutting, sawing, gagging those that screamed, and putting to eternal rest those who dared wake. Pieces of people lined each screen, hollowed out skin shells of torsos stuffed with machinery and stitched together. And yet, the more macabre and decrepit the scene, the more at peace they seemed to be. Every cut was a step and every stitch a twirl. They danced with their hands soaked in blood. Time flickered forward still, and soon they were piecing together something; something that could not be human. It begged for death, and so Number One's short life ended. They sought perfection in their mania. They needed to recreate 'her', their Olive; a daughter born from their own two hands so long ago. They would find the pieces that made her again, they would find a way to bring her back. To bring back the only thing they had loved unconditionally in their twisted lives they were willing to soil a thousand chopping blocks. But they had to be better, Olive had been a mere robot who outgrew her own A.I. and wished for humanity. They intended to give it to her, building a cohesion of man and machine in a continuous stream.

The number eight flashed across the screen, Rain couldn't look away from the ticker-tape horror. She saw herself, her skin stolen and her organs replaced with mechanisms; it was a sight that would prove sour to any constitution. She saw them hold pictures next to her, trying to talk to her, and with little effort at all issuing a disposal order. Rain's pupils shrank, for the first time terror took her face as she struggled to turn her head. Her eyes welled up, her lips forced each and every movement before she froze, she could only let one cry loose from her heart.

"I'm sorry Snow."

Android - The Last Day

Today… Snow didn't come back.

Rain waited and waited, I'm not sure if it's tomorrow yet or not, just that Snow isn't where he's supposed to be. He isn't messing up my hair, hauling bags of stuff into the workshop, or even just telling me stories of how things used to be before either of us were born.

All I have is a note, scribbled worse than me with words that feel wrong, Dee. Words… words Snow shouldn't ever have to say, words that make it seem like… like this isn't just some nightmare

"I'll come back for you, I promise."

Chapter Thirteen - Conniption

Catherine and Catherine had both known a child was impossible, yet each possessed such skill and finesse that they could craft what their bodies denied them. They created Olive from simple parts and a simple frame, yet perhaps most extraordinary was their choice of a blank slate. She was not programmed to love, to care, to speak, or even stand. She would grasp each concept as would a newborn, rapidly growing in knowledge day by day. She proved to be a kind girl, who would wait for both her mother's return each day, not once leaving the apartment many in that same colony would have killed to have. If she looked outside? Her only thoughts were with them, she hoped they were enjoying themselves, she hoped they were happy, she hoped they would be back soon. Her affections could not help but be appreciated; they had what they wanted, a daughter of their own, loving them by choice and not code. Stubborn and firm, but caring twice so. In her they saw the best of humanity, an ironic notion which reality took little time to disprove.

Neither had ever thought much of their own species, their separate journeys into engineering only shadowed that notion even more. One got into more fights as a child than your average tavern drunkard, the other spoke to none but herself and still finding a distaste for the concept. They wanted nothing to do with the world, and less with the people in it. That is, of course until they met. Words were not needed, and a seething hatred was dispelled. Something to live for existed in each other. As one crawled out of her shell, the other lowered her fists and sheathed her fangs. The pendulum clung one last time, never again separating from what it had become. Yet they wanted more, they yearned for the sum of their whole, and Olive had granted it. But she wasn't supposed to, she was an idea, a brief flurry of emotions made solid. She was supposed to be a simple test of their potential, and she surpassed that by measures they could not define.

However, she was not built to last. And she didn't.

Rage found each of them anew, and a perverse passion drove them to try to replace her. They would use every piece down to her joints, but never could they capture even a fragment of that fleeting soul.

They broke.

More than ever, they could deal with no other. Only one another existed in the small world they had retreated into, a small lab where they wouldn't be bound by the morals of others nor the ethics of man. The very same lab where now their bones lay wasting away in a pool of waste as their virtual preservations mocked the lives that stood before them, unaware that they were hurting the closest things to what they had been searching for.

Rain was frozen, whatever will had kept her going for that long had cracked as if it was merely a brittle little biscuit all along. She would not wake again, Usu knew this, he'd heard it a dozen times before coming here, but he wouldn't let her be devoured no matter how far she fell. Ignoring the cackling apparitions, he pulled her limp arm once more, tumbling them both into the muck below. He pulled her from every angle, uncaring for the rips his own body suffered in response. The movement was slow, it was almost futile, but they moved.

Slowly, each body was being brought closer to the entrance as the Catherines commented amongst one another. "It's the wipe isn't it?" "Oh yes, should be a nice blank slate again in no time now." "Ah, those are the best." They somehow allowed a warm smile to breach the cold expanse between them. Their malice was almost as benevolent as it was selfish. They could never see themselves as the cruel monsters others did because they deemed life itself the real monster and everyone else cattle for their scythe. They thought little of Usu's struggle or Rain's demise; thinking of others would hurt too much, thinking of others would remind them of their Olive, and neither had the strength of will for that.

A distance away from Usu's struggle, Mercury and Modbot searched for a way to save Rain on their own, though neither with completely clear motivations. Mercury herself was starting to wonder why she didn't just 'piss the whole thing off' (to put it politely) in the first place, why she felt drawn to their silly little struggle, and perhaps most of all, why Modbot was walking around with only his knees raised above the ground, the rest of his body parallel to the ground in proper limbo fashion.

Feeling the sting of societal judgment as he had come to know so very well, Modbot habitually responded to the awkward silence. "T-This is rather normal you see, or, or certainly more normal than it seems! Due to… a series of unfortunate non-accidental mechanical destructions, I ended up with a pair of barely functioning visual sensors between each knee joint. So while I may be blindfolded from triggering a kill-switch normally, my fogged up knee-eyes can still navigate through most obstacles with pip pip accuracy!"

Mercury was left speechless; disgust and admiration had formed together all at once and the English language along with the art of portmanteau itself wasn't quite prepared to have a word for that feeling just yet. She motioned him to carry on with suspicious eyes and a chromatic hand turn, which his makeshift visual sensors saw as a buffalo eating rice pudding. Thankfully that misinterpretation elicited much the same response, knowing how very un-British of him it would be to disrupt a wild animal's pudding excursion.

Carrying on their own paths, Modbot stumbled across an assortment of spilled paper-clips, a chair, another chair, and then a deviously placed wall. Mercury on the other—somewhat less inept—side of things, was scouring any terminal with power, ripping out drawers and generally having a highly physical debate against office furniture.

"Why not try this office? Looks fancy, dedicated to a chef it is!" Modbot put forth, once again exceeding his own aptitude for helpfulness in times of crisis. The room he'd pointed out was a rather good find, if only for it belonging to a department chief. As he scanned the floor, presumably for more paper-clips, Mercury was brute-forcing her way into the system. Not quite as easy as the others, or one could presume so from her angelic—and frequent—usage of such niceties as "Pig-shit son of a bitch" and "Codflopper!" No one will ever truly know what exactly a 'Codflopper' is, but it evidently lacked positive qualities. Nonetheless, she broke through, if a bit strangely sweatier for the wear.

Everything was there; emails arranging a 'part exchange', a system of some kind between the cybernetics department and the android development wing, instructions to leave a certain bulkhead door sealed at all times, and, while not perfect, a series of blueprints detailing numerous 'failures'. The lacking traits of the latter drew suspicion, as most wouldn't consider 'Looks at me' as grounds for disposal, but then again most people never got close to the technology born between those walls.

It was enough, it had to be. Mercury was running out of time herself, without even being aware of Usu's predicament. Black liquid leaking from underneath her cloak had begun pooling around her feet, the result of over-exerting her efficient yet still fragile construction. Modbot, still currently gifted only in the ways of floor-sight took a quiet note of the liquid, and while he didn't fully understand its meaning, he understood the gravity of the situation. He immediately stood up, ripped off his blindfold and swung Mercury over his shoulder. She told him off for it, maybe half a dozen times, maybe more, but it wasn't nearly enough to phase him at this point.

They were stumbling towards where they had parted with Usu and Rain until finally coming to a scene which washed away any shame Mercury might have accumulated from being carried like a doll. There before them was an open bulkhead door, Usu tugging at Rain's limp body with everything he could muster. Without a word or whisper, suddenly both were suspended in the air by a one-handed raise from Modbot, who couldn't help give a cheeky grin despite circumstances so grim.

"We're getting out of here fluffletuffle, enough time on the floor for both of us I'd say." Those words were almost enough to dull the ache that had overcome Usu's heart, a heart frozen in terror so deeply that the next thing he knew he was back in the bubble and heading out the same tunnel that had drawn them in.

Mercury set the remaining device to give them the directional jolt they needed, though she was coughing badly, her cloak stained from the inside out. Yet she could do more, she could do... something. She looked at Modbot and Usu with deathly sincerity. "Listen, I'll be fine once we reach the top, just need a bit of a recharge, but the girl, she's losing everything right now. Every second is another day she'll never get back. There's something I can do… I didn't want to, but you just better hope Shitbeard doesn't wimp out on you okay? Kick his ass if he gives you trouble, I'll kick it twice for ya myself." She was obviously not well and had passed every limit she'd ever known, but her determination was steadfast as she ripped open the back of Rain's dress and folded her own cloak to shoulder height. "This won't save her, but it will protect whatever she has left, keep it safe you two."

With a few more curse words that felt akin to an ancient spell at this point, she slid her hand inside of Rain's back. Deeper and deeper still, until the top of her right arm fell off and crawled to join its kin. Patterns of grey began appearing and disappearing across Rain's skin until a metal star began rising out of the center of her chest, a single strange gem socketed within. With a comatose breath, Mercury told them, "Take it, and do me a solid by not screwing up this time?" before falling flat herself, her body warping with pain. It was clear now that her cloak was far from simple clothing, it was a prison. The only prison that could keep her whole, and the same one she escaped momentarily to give Usu this final fragment of hope.

He grabbed the gem with no hesitation, holding it tightly to his chest as Rain's body turned cold, brittle and, in one cruel instant, departed his world as dust.

Android - The Day After

I did something horrible Dee.

Something I can't take back, no matter how hard I cry.

I found Snow, in a strange glass thing, holding Usu tightly as he dreamed. The men who took him away said it was a 'cryogenic chamber' and he would sleep a really, really long time, that it's what he wanted. That, if he slept long enough he might be able to help me, but... but that isn't what I wanted! I just wanted him to stay, to stay with me, I don't care how much I forget if we make new memories every day! So I... I hit the glass and... it cracked.

Snow's eyes opened just enough to see me, he was crying just as much as me but for some reason he was smiling. Red lights and bad noises, men were pulling me away but he kept smiling until he fell back to sleep.

They said he might not ever wake up because of what I did, but did you know Dee?

Snow doesn't lie.

I'll wait for him, even if the whole world won't wait with me.

Chapter Fourteen - Silica

The amount of times something as simple as a jewel has held more value than that of a life runs almost innumerable throughout human history. Peasantry and nobility walked fine lines, dotted by mere rocks polished to a sheen. Marriages and life-long bonds formed around the price tag of a controlled commodity, a simple ore in truth. Yet in this strange city built by directionless slaves in honour of their own begotten masters, a small feverish doll in the form of a rabbit held one such mineral, one that truly did carry the weight of a life.

Heavier still by the importance of his charge, Usu held the fragment with both care and terror. He could not lose her, his heart was not built for such woe and with each returning memory he was punishing himself for burdening Rain's heart with just that. What right did he have to make her wait for him? What right did he have to hold everything she was so closely to him?

He didn't, but then again, he didn't need to either.

Love is a devious thing, taking residence in all, whilst paying not a single deposit upfront. Though try as we might to evict, it remains a creature with no boundaries, no borders and most of all, no master. Usu could no more stop Rain's feelings for him than he could stop his for her. Perhaps there was something beautiful about the maddened pair he had just abandoned on the sea floor, after all.

One thing mattered now; he needed to get Rain help. Modbot and Usu were still drenched from their rather unexpected return landing, something largely considered a design flaw in the previously perfected suicide assistance diving bubbles. It was a situation made all the more unusual by it being two in the morning, a time when any decent automation was pretending to be asleep and few doors found themselves open without the use of a particularly violent talent one of them happened to have.

Modbot carried Mercury, or at least tried to do

something resembling that, when in reality it was more a deal of her leaning against him, slumping forward and elbowing him across the face every time he tried to make a comment, pun, or take up more of the burden than was offered. Black ooze was still leaking from both her lips and missing arm but it did little good for her attitude. "Sheesh, you guys move slower than c—" allowing a bit more bile to make its escape, "—congress." An insult that hardly bothered Modbot, who'd long since abandoned his American origins. Now if she'd mentioned Parliament, then he might have a word or two! Those words would be with himself though; both honour and fear prevented him from standing up to her, even when standing itself was the last thing she seemed to be able to do.

Usu looked worried, more worried than by default at least, but his fears were firmly on the little life in his hands. His feelings to Mercury were only that of gratitude. It didn't take much to see that whatever she had done for Rain hurt herself far more than she would ever admit.

After what seemed like hours they at last arrived at Manchester's abode, making an entrance even his false sleep state couldn't ignore. Mercury collapsed the moment they arrived, pushing Modbot to the side and with her one remaining hand slammed the ground with enough force to crack its entirety. Not one for simple physical abuse, she took the opportunity to engage in some father-daughter bonding by yelling, "S-Shitbeard," interrupted by a whimsical bit of passing vomit. "Shitbeard! I brought them back with, with the only information we could find. The girl and I are missing a few pieces though, so could you stop pretending to snore through your ass and do something? Don't make me tell them about what you do with portable air conditioning units, cause you know I wi—"

The last comment had the awkward creature springing immediately to face them, raising as many of his chin-hands to cover Mercury's mouth as he could.

"Hush hush, mah dear, let's have a peek at ye! Missing arm, black stuff that was just laying aroond when ah made ye. Nae good at all!" His eyes surveyed the rest of the room. "Haggisballs looks wrong 'n proper as he ever did, though th' wee rabbit doesn't seem so good, 'n I'd swear thar was yin more o' ye..."

Mercury lashed out, "Bloody hell there was! The girl! The whole reason we went there! I had to preserve her personality and memories in that fragment, and I got a bit of the design data you need. So how about you be less of an ass for once and do something about her would you? We both know how long those things last."

One of his appendages connected to the back of his daughter's neck, the schematics passing over to him in a single heartbeat. He retracted immediately, backing as far up as he could. There wasn't only schematic data in there, but a brutal breakdown of the bodyshop of horrors that made each piece of the puzzle fit. "Gods, well no wonder ah couldnae make ye if ah tried, them bits dinnae grow on trees, and... well actually trees dinnae grow anymore either." Shaking his head for a moment he zipped back down, this time directly in front of Usu. Usu looked at Manchester with broken eyes that spoke of loss. Yet even then, he summoned all his courage as he handed Rain's fragment over, Manchester delicately taking it through a gloved beard hand. "Yer a good laddie ye know, well, a good whatever ye are." Usu found little relief in his praise. "Ah will be straight wi' ye rabbit, ah cannae make her th' same. But ah kin save her, mayhap if th' ghost in th' machine blesses us."

Usu walked closer, nervous and terrified about any possible outcome, until Modbot kneeled down and scuffed up his head. He found strength in that, a strange, perverse head-scruffing fetish sort of strength, but at this point no-one's being picky. Manchester stopped fiddling with some idle calculations and looked at Usu firmly. "In a hundred 'n thirteen years."

Modbot spoke up first. "For what?! For you to twiddle every thumb you've got on that chin of yours?"

Manchester let out another exaggerated sigh, covering the room in a light smog. "Nah, ye blunderbuss. T'save th' lassie. If he kin hold his horses that long, ah kin do something aboot it sure as a catholic's guilt! But..." He leaned ever more forward. "Kin ye hold on that long laddie? Even when ye dinnae ken how for long ye have ta bide? Ah could implant her in a stock model 'n you'd be t'gether fer days at best afore she'd shatter, but if ye take me offer, 'n—more importantly—if it works, th' lassie will be free o' all that wishes ta bind her."

Reality struck Usu straight to the head like so many other things had done on this journey, and while reality was seemingly less physical than a touch screen display panel (for a completely coincidental example), it stung far more. He had no choice; before him was merely the illusion of it. Waiting for her was the only choice he could make even if he lived a thousand lifetimes over. The choice would always be the same. Steeling his heart, he nodded with determination filling both his heart and eyes. Rain had waited for him, waited so much longer, and he could never refuse her the same courtesy.

Modbot looked startled. "Y-You're just going to wait a hundred and thirteen years?" Changing his orientation to the floating Scotsman, he continued. "What even takes that long anyway? You building her a body made from half-burnt Woolworth's coupons?"

Manchester was already busying himself after witnessing Usu's resolve; half his body was stitching up Mercury while the other half kept flipping through thousands of schematics, but he did say this much, "Nae at a', that wouldn't! Ah will have ta grow it, hoping it steals shape from whatever auld memr'es o' her are left in this wee pebble. 'N ye rabbit, you'll need ta be thar when she wakes up, ta remind her o' wha' she was, 'n help her become what she wants ta be."

With those simple, barely intelligible words, time was forgotten. Minutes became months and hours fell ill without hegemony.

The world withered as it always had, and a small white rabbit slumped against a massive watery chamber for much of it. He would not look, he would not fear, and he would not count.

He would only wait.

Years, decades, and a full century scattered around him, blossoming only his regret for making Rain experience that same wait he now did. But it was all he could do, and all he could promise this girl he held so dearly. He didn't care if she looked the same, or even if she remembered him, he felt the world needed someone like her in it, and his world might as well not exist without her.

Eventually even thought became secondary, nothing could move him anymore. No matter the visitor, he lay motionless, every ounce of his life hoping for the one behind him. Hoping she could try and sneak in his bed again at night, and that he could bring her joy with tinkered toys of delight. He wanted to see her scream at a book for being too long, and then cry because it never should have ended.

His nearly lifeless body, long since numb from the cold of the glass he rested against, shuddered. Mere moments later, glass and water crashed around him, scattering like the petals of lost civilisation they were. Two arms wrapped around his chest from behind, and before his fraying body could turn in even the slightest, a wet head was touching his own. There was a small giggle, a forced back tear and one little girl could only whisper, "I missed you."

Side Story - Gain

You, as a completely normal individual, may at times find yourself wondering a fair deal of things. Does that sandwich taste better upside down? Which way is upside down? Is lithium an acceptable seasoning?

Contending that you might not be a perfectly normal addict however, and thus a reader instead, makes for far more complicated questions. Just what did Modbot do all those narratively-truncated years in which Rain spent incubating? Did Mercury's arm ever get repaired?

Modbot spent many of the first few years watching over Usu and Rain, occasionally making sure Manchester wasn't trying to retrofit their internals into musical instruments. Mercury on the other—previously dismembered—hand, tried her best to keep everything business as usual. Her father was far too preoccupied with staring at an artificial growth chamber to bother with her rather urgent repairs. Yet the quasi-legal body part industry would wait for no man, no woman, and certainly not one with the forceful demeanor of Mercury.

Of course, she was smart enough to string together a collection of replacement arms on her own. Her chambers quickly became lined in enough right arms to cause even her father's chin to quiver perplexedly. For fun, she'd try cannibalizing one every now and then, which had less of a regrowth effect than it had terrifying a certain all-purpose janitorial robot that may or may not have wandered into her chambers one particularly dull day.

"Right, I saw that! You can say whatever you like, butter me up with all your posh curse words, but I definitely just saw you eat that vintage nursing-unit arm!"

Wires still slurping into the abyss of her shawl, Mercury simply replied, "Bleeding hell, it's been twenty-five years already, get a hobby!"

Modbot, not to be outdone by anything other than everything, was quick to proudly retort, "This is my hobby!" before realising that it didn't quite come out as empowering as he had imagined it would. "I thought about it you know."

"About what?" In a rare compromise from Mercury, she feigned ignorance to continue some semblance of a conversation.

"Heading back to New York, cleaning some more things, shouting at stainless steel for being stainless. But is that what really matters in the grand scheme of things? You lost your arm and gained a fetish, whereas I almost paid attention to the plot. I'd say we both wagered an awful lot not to see this through."

"Wait wait, paying attention to the world around you does *not* equate to liquidating my fucking arm several meters below sea level. These aren't fetishes either, they're, they're… options!" Mercury quickly blurted.

"Options? You mean breakfast, brunch, lunch, and dinner? I suppose you're at least getting some variety in your diet."

"Not the point you copper cockatrice! We were breaching meaningful territory here, about our lives or lack thereof, and there you go obsessing about one little arm that happens to be digestible. Would it make you feel more comfortable if I said your right arm is particularly unappetizing?" Her words hurt Modbot in a profoundly deep way that we're not really going to pay any attention to at all, but you should keep in mind they did. He'd never been especially proud of his right arm, but he'd at least always thought it edible! The revelation shook the foundations of his artificial confidence scripts.

This sort of banter wasn't exactly new ground for either of them. The years and even decades flew by, but neither would rightly admit how they longed for those brief days together. Modbot, out of pride and Mercury, presumably because she was either too busy stealing limbs or nonchalantly consuming them. Still, every morning she'd secretly watch over Usu and the seed of flesh behind his furry, broken body, threatening accidental murder against

Manchester whenever he had inspirational ideas that might rightfully muck things up.

They'd lost track long ago, just how long had they spent their days watching over him? Bickering and bantering through twilight hours, each had grown accustomed to the other, and despite their engineered differences, a common hope kept a flame inside each of them bright, unwavering against the winds of time.

Neither had a reason to care, neither was supposed to have the circuitry for it in the first place, but strangely akin to neuroplasticity in the rather dead humans around them, they found themselves rewriting their own principals during their journey. Granted, things like recreational cannibalism and the mounting of random objects to one's chassis might not be the best examples of where that road had lead them, but it was a road few of their kind had ever walked, and one that even humanity had struggled to find in the mists and muck of their own undoing.

Not being the editor who insisted on the creation of a side story, you may find yourself between a rock and a bored place right now. The rock was put there to bludgeon yourself with, the bored place a rather apologetic burial mound for your expectations. Though before you cover yourself with that last patch of proverbial dirt, I should make it clear that all hope for a worthwhile narrative was not quite yet lost.

Rain, or at least what claimed to be her, was changing by the day, reflecting the memories of the one who waited for her. The gem Mercury sacrificed part of herself to create, the shield for her persona, had long since come undone. Fragments adorning the edges of her tiny body, finally taking shape after countless years of dormancy.

With but a breath they anatomically could not possibly have had, both Modbot and Mercury finally found themselves possessed by the same forces of stagnation that held Usu so tightly. Even if their feelings could not compare to his, they found a synthetic synchronicity, and a dull ache replaced their curiosity.

They watched.

They waited.

And in an instant, a small familiar frame rejected the glass that bound it, broke free from the curse of time and whispered life back into Usu's forlorn figure.

About the Author

Jayde Ver Elst is a critically-ignored author with an unrivalled track record of not being set on fire by his reader base. Specialising in sloppy wit and emotional trickery, he's almost certain to have been accidentally murdered by someone once you've read this.

About the Cover Artist

Moa Wallin is a Swedish artist and illustrator. Her detailed and imaginative paintings walk the line between the adorable and the absurd, occasionally tipping over to either side.

To see more of Moa's work, visit her website at www.moawallin.com

www.ingramcontent.com/pod-product-compliance
Lightning Source LLC
Chambersburg PA
CBHW020615120726
47905CB00003B/806